The Savage Life 2

Lock Down Publications and
Ca$h Presents
The Savage Life 2
A Novel by **J-Blunt**

Lock Down Publications

P.O. Box 870494
Mesquite, Tx 75187

Visit our website
www.lockdownpublications.com

Lock Down Publications
Like our page on Facebook: Lock Down Publications @
www.facebook.com/lockdownpublications.ldp
Cover design and layout by: **Dynasty Cover Me**
Book interior design by: **Shawn Walker**
Edited by**: Lauren Burton**

Stay Connected with Us!

Text **LOCKDOWN** to 22828 to stay up-to-date
with new releases, sneak peeks, contests and more…

Submission Guideline.

Submit the first three chapters of your completed manuscript to ldpsubmissions@gmail.com, subject line: Your book's title. The manuscript must be in a .doc file and sent as an attachment. The document should be in Times New Roman, double-spaced and in size 12 font. Also, provide your synopsis and full contact information. If sending multiple submissions, they must each be in a separate email.

Have a story but no way to send it electronically? You can still submit to LDP/Ca$h Presents. Send in the first three chapters, written or typed, of your completed manuscript to:

LDP: Submissions Dept
Po Box 870494
Mesquite, Tx 75187

DO NOT send original manuscript. Must be a duplicate.

Provide your synopsis and a cover letter containing your full contact information.

Thanks for considering LDP and Ca$h Presents.

J-Blunt

Prologue

Knock, knock, knock!

Reese got up from the couch, shaking dreadlocks from his face as he limped to the door. "Who dat?"

"It's Dirty. Is Chante here?"

Reese opened the door and seen a tall, muscular, dark-skinned nigga standing on the front porch. He was bald headed with a full beard and looked to be in his late thirties. "Who is you?"

"I'm Dirty. Where Chante?" he asked, expressing his impatience with an audible breath.

Reese could sense the man's hostility. Wanting to protect his girlfriend, he became more inquisitive. "How you know my girl?"

Dirty mugged him, tired of the questions. "Is Chante in that house?" Chante used to be his girl. That was before he went to prison seven years ago. While he was locked up, she broke bad and ran away with his paper. Now that he was free, he wanted his money back. Every single penny.

Reese returned the mug. "Yeah, she here. Fuck you want wit' my girl, nigga?"

The chrome .45 was in Dirty's hand in an instant. He slapped Reese across the face with the hand cannon, knocking him to the ground. Before Reese knew what was happening, Dirty grabbed him by the dreads and dragged him into the house. Two women were sitting on the living room couch. he daughter was Cherry, a twenty-two-year-old stripper. When they seen Dirty dragging Reese by the hair, they screamed.

"Shut the fuck up!" Dirty yelled, pointing his gun at the women. After letting go of Reese's hair, he walked to stand in front of Chante. "You thought I was gon' forget about how you did me?"

The woman looked like she'd seen a ghost. "Dirty, what's going on, man? When you get out?"

"Fuck when I got out. Bitch, where my money?"

"Um, I-I don't got no money," she stuttered. "I don't know what you talking about."

He pointed the gun at her boyfriend's leg and squeezed the trigger. *Pop*!

"Ah!" Reese screamed.

Dirty pointed the gun at the young woman next to Chante. "What up, Cherry? You know I got love for you, right? But if yo' momma lie to me again, I'm blowing yo' brains out."

"C'mon, Monte. Don't do this. Please," Chante begged, tears streaming down her face. "I don't have it. I don't know where to get fifty thousand dollars."

"Fucked up it had to end like this. All you had to do was keep it gutta." Dirty Monte put the chrome .45 Smith and Wesson to Chante's head.

"Wait!" the daughter called. "Wait! Don't shoot my mother. I might know a way to get you the money."

He turned to look at Cherry. "I'm listening."

"I know a nigga that got money. I can tell you how to get at 'im, but you gotta take it."

He laughed. "You think I'm stupid, bitch? Think you finna get me set up? Hell nah."

"I'm not playing, Dirty. I wouldn't do you like that. I know you don't fuck around. I remember how you did niggas when I was little, and what they used to say about you. I'm not playing."

He gave Cherry a long stare before lowering the pistol. "A'ight. Talk."

"The nigga is Black Stacks. His name not that big in Minneapolis, but he having it."

"You know where he keep the bag?"

"Not everything. I know a house he used to stash shit in. Money, guns, and drugs."

Dirty turned to Reese. "Get to know my name and face, nigga. Next time you see me, move the fuck out the way. And tell all these bitch-ass fuck-niggas that Dirty Monte back, and I want reparations. C'mon Cherry."

***

"Who was that nigga that answered the door? He said he was yo' mama boyfriend."

"Yeah, that's Reese. She been fucking with him for a couple years."

"Is he somebody out here? Who he fuck with?"

"Nobody really. He not plugged or nothing. He moved from down south a couple years ago. I don't think you gotta worry 'bout him hittin' back or calling the police. My momma know the game."

He glanced over, checking her out. Cherry was beauty queen fine. Dark chocolate skin, thick and curvy frame, big titties, and a cute face. The long weave ponytail hung to the middle of her back. She wore a tight red dress that hugged her curves like a glove.

"How you know I was thinking about all that?"

She smiled a little. "I'm not a little girl no more. I know how it is out here. I fuck wit' street niggas."

He shook his head. "That's crazy."

"When you get out, Dirty? Why you just now coming around?" Cherry asked as she drove along the interstate in her gray Chevrolet Equinox.

"Got out yesterday. Been thinking about seein' yo' mama for seven years. She bogus for how she did a nigga. I thought she was my bitch. Gon' leave me on stuck like that after I was good to her? She lucky I didn't shoot her ass," he vented.

"I remember how you was. I used to hear stories 'bout how crazy you was, but you was good to me. I was too young to understand everything and why she did what she did, but I remember you used to buy me everything I asked for."

He smiled. "Yeah, I did spoil you, huh? That's 'cause I didn't have no kids, and you was cool," he said, taking a quick glance at her thick thighs.

She caught him checking her out. "I see you looking, nigga. You don't gotta be shy about it."

"Nah, it ain't like that. It just been a minute," he explained. It felt funny checking her out. He'd known her since she was a shorty.

"I know. Seven years a long time. I know it felt good getting pussy again."

"Damn, baby. When the fuck you get so bold?"

"I told you, I fuck with street niggas. And I dance at Vixens. I'm all about my coins. You didn't even have to shoot Reese. If you woulda told me you needed a way to get a bag, I woulda put you on Black Stacks out the gate."

He shook his head. "Damn. It's crazy how everything changed since I went in. You sound like a savage."

She nodded. "Like I told you, I'm 'bout my money."

"A'ight. Tell me about the house we going to."

"It's one of Black safe houses. I came over here two or three times to fuck him and get some money. He normally keep a flunky or two in there. JT or Relo. They know who I am."

He eyed her again, trying to read her. "You know if you fuck me over, I'm killing everybody you know?"

She took her eyes off the highway to meet his stare. "I'm not on bullshit, Dirty. It's these niggas or my mama. I know what it is."

He nodded. "A'ight. Go in there and give me a lay of the land. I'ma wait outside."

"I got a better idea. I'ma go in there and see what's going on. If I think you can make the move, I'ma send you a text. I need yo' phone number."

"I don't got no phone."

"Okay. Keep mine. I'ma use one of theirs."

Ten minutes later, Cherry parked the SUV at the curb of the brown and white safe house on Minneapolis's northwest side. The night was dark and the block looked deserted. Cherry strolled up the walkway with purpose and knocked on the door.

"Who is it?" a man called from the inside.

"Cherry. Where is Black?"

When the door opened, a short, light-skinned nigga with long dreads looked her from head to toe. "What up, shawty? He ain't here."

"Hey, Relo. Do you know when he coming back?"

"Nah. I ain't heard from the nigga all day."

"Damn. Can I use yo' phone? This bitch-ass nigga took mine. I need to call a ride."

He opened the door to let her in. "Yeah. Come in. What happened? Who you get into it with?"

"Trick-ass nigga Fresh. Nigga mad 'cause I don't want him to be my boyfriend. I ain't looking for no man. I'm chasin' this money. Who all here with you?"

He grabbed the phone off the table and handed it to her. "Nobody. JT probably come through later."

"What's the address here? I'ma send my girlfriend a text."

"If you need a ride, I got you. Or you can chill with me and we can smoke something."

She raised an eyebrow, sending the text. "You know I'm

'bout my coins, baby boy. Don't be playing with me like that."

He smiled, wanting some pussy. "Shit, I got whatever you talkin' 'bout. You know that."

Cherry dropped the phone on the table and straddled his lap, hiking the dress above her hips. "Gimme two dollars and you can have whatever you like," she whispered, kissing him on the lips.

Relo's hands found her phatty and squeezed. It was jiggly, soft, and got his dick so hard it threatened to bust through his pants. "I got you, baby. Let me see what that head game like."

Cherry dropped to her knees, freeing his dick and going to work. She bobbed her head up and down, using lots of spit as she sucked.

The head was so good that Relo closed his eyes. He didn't open them again until he heard the front door open. He forgot to lock it, and it was too late to do anything about it. Dirty was already in the living room with the .45 pointed at his chest.

"You know what this is, nigga. Gimme what chu got, and what chu don't got, you can keep!"

Relo's hands flew in the air. "Ain't nothin' in here, brah."

"Move, baby girl," Dirty said, pushing Cherry out of the way and shooting Relo on the leg.

Pop!

"Ah, shit!"

"Lie to me again and I'ma burn yo' bitch-ass. Where the shit at, nigga?"

"Okay! A'ight! It's a safe in the room."

"Get up, nigga. Show me where it at."

Relo struggled from the couch and limped to the room. Dirty was on his heels. The safe was in the closet, top shelf. After popping it open, Dirty grabbed the money inside, all twenty-five thousand in cash.

"That's all we got in here," Relo groaned, holding his bleeding leg.

Dirty nodded before lifting the pistol to Relo's face. "Got er'thang we need. Good looking."

Pop!

***

"How much do I get of that?" Cherry asked, watching the road while Dirty counted the money.

"Yo' mama still owe me twenty-five racks."

"C'mon now, Dirty. I did what I could. And you wouldn't have nothing if it wasn't for me. We don't gotta split it, but give a bitch something and I might be able to find you another lick."

He laughed, tossing her five Gs. "I'm just fuckin' with you, baby girl. You know I can't tell you no. You did good. Seem like you got this jack shit in yo' blood."

"I told you, I'm 'bout my coins," she smiled. "You remember what I asked you earlier about getting some pussy? You got some yet?"

An image of her sucking Relo's dick played in his mind. "Nah. I slept on my sister's couch last night watching porn on the phone," he chuckled.

"Let's get a bottle and a room. I can show you how a real bitch do a real nigga. What my mom did to you was foul. Let me make it up to you."

After stopping to get a bottle of Remy Martin and a quarter ounce of weed, they started the party in the truck. By the time they checked into the hotel room, they were good and tipsy.

"Sit back and let me take care of you," Cherry said, pushing him in the chair.

Dirty sat back, smoking a blunt and drinking from the bottle of Remy. Cherry performed a sexy strip tease. When all her clothes were off, she move in front of him, doing the splits and twerking. Then she got up from the floor and lay on the bed, opening her legs and rubbing her bald pussy. She fingered herself while rubbing her clit, putting on a erotic self pleasure show.

Dirty's dick was so hard it hurt. When he couldn't take it no more, he stripped and walked to the edge of the bed, holding his dick like it was a sword. Cherry got on her knees and took him down her throat, sucking on him like his dick was a popsicle. After all those years without pussy, Dirty was a born-again virgin. He busted in less than a minute, filling her mouth with so much nut she couldn't swallow it all. It dripped from the sides of her mouth. And being a professional man-pleaser, she kept right on sucking.

Dirty reached around and stuck two fingers in her ass and two in her pussy, fingering her roughly as she chewed him. His second nut came almost as quickly as the first.

After filling her mouth again, he flipped her on her back, spreading her legs and letting his tongue go to work on that pussy. He spread her lips apart, using his tongue like a dildo, and made her go crazy. Then he began sucking her clit while fingering her in the ass. Cherry came in waves, wetting his face with her juices. Feeling like a freak, he let his tongue slip down to her ass and go to work. He sucked and licked her sphincter like it was a clitoris, driving the young stripper wild. After she came again, he pushed her knees to her chest and beat the pussy up.

They would remember the fuck session for a long time. When they were done, Dirty and Cherry lay back and got high.

"Damn, Cherry. You done grew the fuck up, for real!"

"I told you I know how to treat a real nigga. And damn, you can fuck, nigga. That fresh-outta-jail dick is the truth!"

"That was years of pent-up frustration. Let me see yo' phone real quick so I can call my sister. She was supposed to look into something for me."

Cherry grabbed her phone from the table and handed it to him. "What you want me to do with Relo phone?"

"I gotta take out that SIM card and get rid of it. Then I'ma throw it away. Can't let twelve see that last text," he told her before making the call to his sister. "What up, April? This, Dirty. Was you able to find Eddie?"

"Yeah. I got the number for you. He live in Milwaukee."

"In Milwaukee?" Dirty frowned. "Fuck he doing in Wisconsin?"

"I don't know. But he waiting on you to call him."

After getting Eddie's number, he called his cousin.

"Yeah?" a deep voice answered.

"Is this Eddie?"

"Yeah. Who dis?"

"What up, fool-ass nigga? This Dirty."

Eddie's voice rose a couple octaves. "What up, nigga? April called and told me you was out. What you on?"

"Shit. Trynna get my shit together. How the fuck you end up in Wisconsin?"

"Shit, I was over here eatin' 'til my nigga, Monster, got killed. Now we trynna get these bitch-ass jackboys. Call theyself Savages. Niggas put fifty on each one of they heads."

That got Dirty's attention. "Fifty Gs? How many niggas you talkin' 'bout?"

"It's four of them ho-ass niggas. And they all gotta go."

Dirty turned to Cherry. "How you feel about catching a plane to Wisconsin?"

J-Blunt

Chapter 1

The devastation Dro felt inside couldn't be expressed with words. Asia was gone. A single bullet to the head ended the innocent life that had just begun. Nothing he'd been through in life had prepared him for the pain that threatened to undo his sanity. He could feel the darkness overtaking his soul. Nothing mattered anymore. He didn't care about money. He didn't care about leaving the streets for a better life. He didn't care about his relationship with Forever. And He didn't care about all the ways God protected and warned him. All he cared about was bringing pain on the nigga that killed his daughter.

He'd already cried all the tears, shed so many his tear ducts didn't work anymore. Blackness covered his heart. Dread surrounded him. And the only thoughts he wanted to think were those of vengeance.

The hospital room's door opened and America stumbled in, drunk from the devastation, tears dripping down her face. "What happened to my baby, Dro? Why you let them kill our baby?" she cried, collapsing to the floor.

There was a time when America's pain would have had an effect on him, would've made him feel some form of sympathy, but the empathetic part of him died with Asia. Seeing America sprawled on the floor, crying her eyes out was disgusting. And the fact she was putting the blame on him pissed him off.

"Get the fuck outta my room," he said coldly.

She looked up, anger and hysteria swirling in her brown eyes. "You got her killed, nigga! It's yo' fault. I know them niggas was looking for you."

The words burned in his chest like someone had poked him with a hot cattle prod. If he could've gotten up from the bed, he would've beat her ass. But the surgery wounds on his back and legs confined him. Instead of kicking her ass, he grabbed the nearest object – a flower pot on the bedside table – and threw it at her.

"Bitch, get the fuck outta here! Get the fuck out!"

The pot missed. Dirt and ceramic shards sprayed America, but she didn't move from the floor. Her limbs didn't work. She lay there crying.

"You got our baby killed, Dro. I hate you. I hate you so much."

"What's going on in here?" a nurse asked, rushing into the room. When she seen America on the floor crying, surrounded by dirt, she dropped down to console the grief-stricken woman. "Ma'am, are you okay?"

"Get that bitch out my room. I want her up outta here!" Dro barked, showing no sympathy.

"He got our daughter killed! He killed our baby!" America cried.

Dro grabbed the IV bag, snatching the needle from his arm, and threw it at America. *"Get that bitch outta here! Get that bitch out!"* he screamed.

"Calm down, Ruben! I'm moving her," the nurse said, helping America stand. "Ma'am, you have to get up. C'mon. Let me get you out of here."

"He got my baby killed. He killed my baby," America whined as she was led from the room.

Dro lay back in bed, ignoring the blood running down his arm. The IV needle had cut him good. America's words bounced around in his head like beads inside a baby rattle. She was partially right. His dirty deeds had come back to bite him in the most unimaginable way. Never in a million years did he think what he did in the streets would affect someone he loved. But it had. Now someone had to pay.

When the doors opened again, the nurse that took America from the room walked back in with another nurse. "Ruben, I'm nurse Megan. Are you okay?" she asked, picking the IV bag up from the floor. Her coworker cleaned up the broken plant and dirt.

"Yeah," he mumbled.

"We need to replace the IV. There are antibiotics inside that you need. You just had surgery, and you need this."

"A'ight."

After grabbing supplies from the cabinet, the women worked in tandem, cleaning the blood and putting the needle back into his arm.

"You know it's not your fault, right?" Megan asked, looking sympathetic.

He gave her a look that would scare the devil. "Mind yo' business, lady."

The look shook both women. "Okay. Well, we'll be outside. Hit the call button if you need anything."

"I'm good. Just leave me alone."

The women left, but Megan returned twenty minutes later. "I know you said to leave you alone, but she insisted on seeing you."

Dro looked and seen Forever being wheeled into the room. She wore a blue gown and held onto the IV bag on wheels. Her face normally brought some kind of joy, but not today. Seeing her in the wheelchair added to the guilt. She had been hurt because of his dirty deeds.

"I said I didn't want no company. Take her out."

The nurse looked caught between a rock and a hard place.

"It's okay," Forever told her. "I got it from here. You can leave."

Megan remembered what happened when America was in the room. "Are you sure? He is really agitated."

"I'm sure. We'll be fine."

After one last look, the nurse left.

Forever wheeled herself in front of the bed and they stared at one another. "How are you?" she asked.

"I don't wanna talk to nobody, Forever. Leave me alone," he groaned.

"After everything we've been through, you're going to treat me like this? You can't just dismiss me."

"What the fuck you want me to say? That I'm okay? I'm not. My mu'fuckin' daughter just died."

The words felt like punches, making Forever flinch. "I know, Ruben. And I'm sorry. But shutting me out won't help. I'm your girl. I got shot, too. We will get through this together."

"Just leave me alone, Forever. You see what happened to you and my cousin. Ain't nobody around me safe. Just leave. Let me get through this."

"Are you breaking up with me?"

Dro closed his eyes for a moment, letting out a long breath. "Yeah. Now get out."

Forever got loud. "No! I'm not going anywhere! I got shot in the back, and now you expect me to leave? Hell no! You can't do this. We're going to get through this. God will bring us through. Don't lose your faith, Ruben."

"God?" Dro mugged. "You wanna talk about God? For real? God just let my daughter and my cousin die. I came to Him. I got baptized. I asked for forgiveness. I changed. And this what I get? I ain't trynna hear that God shit."

"No, Ruben. Don't say that, baby. Don't stop trusting in God. We have to lean on him, baby. We have –"

"*Ask God why the fuck he take my daughter!*" Dro exploded. "I don't wanna hear that shit. I'ma be my own God. I'ma do what the fuck I want. I'ma find the niggas that did this shit and kill they whole mu'fuckin' family. That's what I want, Forever. Now, pray to God to give me that."

Pain filled her tear-soaked eyes. "No, Ruben. Don't let the devil win. Let God fight your battle. Don't make the situation worse, baby."

Dro didn't respond. He was done talking about and hearing about God.

Forever wheeled to the bedside and grabbed his hand. "Ruben, please talk to me. Don't shut me out, baby."

He snatched away from her. "I don't want to talk, Forever. I want to be left alone."

"Okay. I'm going to sit here with you. We don't have to talk, but I'm not leaving."

Commotion near the door made them look up. "Hey! You guys can't go in there! Immediate family only!" a nurse called.

"Fuck that shit! Where my nigga at?" Tae yelled, walking in the room. He was followed by the Savages.

"Dro, you good, nigga?" Twenty asked as they rushed to the bedside.

"Bitch-ass niggas killed my baby," Dro moaned.

"You guys can't be in here!" Nurse Megan said. "If you don't leave, I'm calling security."

"Bitch, we don't give a fuck about yo' security!" Lunatic mugged.

"These my brothers," Dro spoke up. "They immediate family. They good."

Megan looked at all the men skeptically. "Ruben, you can only have immediate family right now."

"Didn't he just tell you we his brothers, bitch?" Tae spat.

"These my brothers," Dro repeated. "They good."

The nurse gave them all suspicious looks before leaving.

"Tell us who did this shit and we gon' fuck them niggas

over," Twenty promised.

Dro looked at Forever. "Get out."

"No. I told you I'm not leaving."

Tae grabbed the handles on her wheelchair and rolled her toward the door. "Yes, you is. You gotta get the fuck outta here."

She tried to put up a fight. "No! Let my chair go! Stop!"

Twenty walked over to open the door and help Tae push her out of the room. "My bad, shorty, but you can't be in here right now. Come back later."

After pushing Forever from the room, the Savages gathered around the bed.

"What happened, nigga. Who did this shit?" Lunatic asked.

"Tulip nigga. I seen his bitch-ass at the strip club the night you got bail, but I wasn't sure who he was. Twenty, remember the nigga I asked you about? Black-ass nigga with the fish eyes and scar on his face?"

Twenty nodded. "Yeah. I remember that shit. Damn, that was his bitch-ass?"

"Yeah. Nigga caught me at the State Fair wit' my girls. I think it was a humbug. Bitch-ass nigga killed my baby and my cousin. Shot me and Forever."

"Where you hit at?" Tae asked, looking him over.

"Hit me twice in the back and twice in the back of my legs."

"Damn, my nigga. We gon' get that bitch. That's my word," Lunatic promised.

"Don't do shit 'til I get out the hospital," Dro said. "I wanna be there. And I wanna kill them niggas' whole family. Kids and all. Mammas and daddies. Not just Tulip baby daddy, but the niggas that was with him, too. All them pussy-niggas' whole families gotta go."

"Say no more. I'ma holla at Whisper and see if he can put a word out about these niggas. They from Chicago, and if they plugged, we might be able to find out who they is."

The door opening made the Savages turn and look. Two police officers walked in wearing hostile looks. "Gentlemen, we're going to have to ask you to leave the patient's room," one of them spoke, resting a hand on the butt of his service pistol.

"So, this what y'all on?" Tae asked.

"Why we gotta leave?" Twenty asked. "We didn't do nothing."

"The only people allowed to visit the patient right now are immediate family members."

"We his brothers," Lunatic said.

"Actually, we know that you're not. Mr. Patrick, your mother and father are down the hall waiting with your sisters. Gentlemen, I'm going to have to ask you to leave. Say your goodbyes. It's time for you to go."

"A'ight, Dro. We gone. Love, nigga. Stay dangerous," Tae said before the Savages left the room. The police following behind them.

"Ruben, are you okay?" Marcia cried as she ran into the room, followed by Lenny, Kailah, and Shanice.

"I'm good," he said flatly.

"We seen America. They said Asia didn't make it," Lenny said, tears rolling down his face.

Dro shook his head, fighting back the pain. "She gone. Savannah, too."

"Oh, God, no!" Marcia cried.

The family stood around the bed crying while Dro remained stoic. "Hang in there, son," Lenny said, patting him on the shoulder. "God gon' bring us through this. You gon' be okay."

***

One Week Later

The Savages sat inside Tae's Tahoe, looking around hyper-vigilantly. They kept hands on their pistols, watching their little brother's back. Dro limped from the SUV, using the crutches to keep balance. He walked up to the dilapidated and abandoned house, making his way to the back door.

"Uncle Crush! Crush!"

A few moments later the back door opened and an older, disheveled man walked outside. "Hey, nephew. Man, what's up with you and the crutches? I thought you was done with the street life? Don't tell me you backslid," he laughed.

Dro's face remained serious. "It's all bad, Unc. They killed our daughters."

Crush's face slowly transformed from a joking demeanor to serious. "What you just say? Who daughter you talking about?"

"I'm talking about Savannah and Asia. They shot me up while we was at the State Fair. They killed our daughters."

Crush grabbed the doorframe to steady himself, a look of disbelief flashing across his face. "Your Asia and my Savannah? How? This don't make no sense."

"I took Asia and Forever to the State Fair. We ran into Candice and yo' daughters. This nigga, J-Mac, and his niggas shot us up. Asia and Savannah died."

Crush collapsed, grabbing his chest. "Nah, nephew. You bullshitting. Tell me this is some bullshit."

Seeing the pain on his uncle's face was torture. "I'm not bullshitting. They gone."

Sobs wracked Crush's body as he wept. "No, God! Why?

Aw, nah!"

"Don't trip, Unc. Somebody gon' pay for this. I promise."

J-Blunt

Chapter 2

"Bass, you see me shining, nigga?" KC called, holding a bottle of Rosé in the air while a thick and curvaceous stripper danced on his lap. KC was with The Drama Boyz, a group of shooters that put in work all over the city. They had their hands in everything from trapping to guns for hire.

"Ain't nothing like having money, nigga!" Bass bragged, adjusting the Cartier frames on his face while watching a woman do tricks on a pole. The Drama Boyz were riding around in a party bus, enjoying the fruits if their hard work in the streets.

"On God, I'm the truth! I can fuck off twenty racks and not even blink!" Duke bragged as he showered a nearby dancer with dollar bills.

"Make sure you tell yo' bitches how The Drama Boyz go hard. I might fuck a bitch and pay a bill!" Playboy sang, holding his phone up to record everything on Facebook live.

The party bus pulled to a stop at a red light, everyone aboard oblivious to the danger that lurked in the black Buick Regal trailing behind. Four killers watched the bus intently, waiting on their moment to strike. They were on a busy street and didn't want to be recorded by the many traffic cameras attached to street lights. So they waited. When the light turned green, the hunt continued.

"Listen up, y'all! Check it out," Playboy called, getting everyone's attention. "I wanna have a contest and post this shit. Right now. I want my dick sucked, and I got a band for whatever one of y'all can make one of The Drama Boyz bust a nut the fastest."

Greed shown in the three strippers' eyes.

"Shit, you ain't said nothing, nigga. Who want they dick sucked by the baddest lips in the city?" Chardonnay asked, eyeing the clique of niggas like they were snacks.

"Quit talkin' 'bout it," Playboy said, unbuckling his Gucci belt. When he looked at his niggas and seen they weren't getting ready to get head, he mugged them. "What you niggas doin'? Y'all ain't heard what I just said? Y'all don't want y'all dicks sucked?"

"Hell yeah!" his niggas called.

"You bitches come get this band!" Playboy waved.

Chardonnay dropped to her knees and quickly sucked Playboy's dick into her mouth. Wanting their pockets to be a thousand dollars fatter, the other women followed suit, dropping before The Drama Boyz and letting their lips go to work. Playboy live streamed it all.

"Aw, shit! Damn!" KC groaned as one of the strippers brought him to a quick climax.

"Gimme that stack, nigga!" Carmel celebrated, opening wide to show her cum stained tongue.

"Damn! Ol' virgin-ass nigga!" Playboy clowned. "Yo' uncircumcised li'l dick-ass ain't even last two minutes."

Chardonnay moved her head. The contest was over.

"Hold on, baby. I didn't bust yet," Playboy said, pushing her head back down. "I got a blue note for you. G'on, take care of that. And I got that stack for you, Carmel. Y'all gon' finish showing me and my niggas a good time."

The bus atmosphere quickly changed from a party vibe to a sexual one as the strippers and goons got down and gritty.

"Ladies and gentlemen, we're at the hotel," the bus driver called, parking in the lot and watching the show in the rearview mirror.

"A'ight. Go grab a room for us. Here we come," Playboy said, drilling Chardonnay's phat ass from the back, not yet ready to leave until he busted a nut.

After a little hesitation, the bus driver was able to tear his eyes away from the live sex show. He went inside the hotel to get his riders a room.

While he was inside, the killers struck. The Savages left the Buick, armed with automatic weapons, racing toward the party bus. Tae and Twenty went to the passenger door and looked inside. The orgy was in full swing, and nobody noticed the peepers. Dro and Lunatic went to the driver's door and climbed inside, their pistols drawn.

Duke noticed them first, but it was already too late.

Clap, clap, clap, clap, clap, clap, clap, clap, clap!

Pop, pop, pop, pop, pop, pop, pop, pop, pop, pop!

Screams from men and women were drowned out by gunfire. No one was left alive. And just to make sure they were all dead, Dro walked around and stood over everybody to shoot them in the head or face five more times.

"They all gone, dawg," Lunatic called, ready to leave the grisly murder scene. "Let's go."

"I only got a couple more," he mumbled, standing over KC and tearing his face apart with bullets.

Lunatic got off the bus and went to join Tae and Twenty in the getaway car.

"Fuck the nigga doin'?" Tae asked, ready to go.

"He standing over everybody and giving 'em facials. Nigga tripping, brah. We gotta get the fuck outta here," Lunatic said, looking around nervously.

Dro had just stepped from the bus when he noticed the driver a few feet away, a horrified look on his face. Feeling the need to kill everything with a breath, Dro lifted the Glock, squeezing the trigger until the man was on the ground. Wanting to give him the same fate as his passengers, Dro walked over and shot him in he face twice before jogging to the Regal.

"Fuck wrong wit' chu, nigga?" Tae asked, speeding away

from the scene.

"Had to make sure er'body was dead," Dro answered flatly, face and voice devoid of any emotions.

Lunatic snatched off the mask angrily. "All them niggas was dead. You on some bullshit, nigga."

Dro got mad and raised his voice. "Fuck them niggas! They killed Rich Boy and put Trouble in a wheelchair. Them pussy mu'fuckas got what the fuck they had coming."

"That ain't the point," Twenty spoke up. "We just made that move in a hotel parking lot. We was trynna get in and out, not stand around and overkill er'body and risk gettin' caught."

"That's why we wore masks. We ain't get caught. We gettin' away right now. You niggas trippin' over nothing," Dro said, blowing them off.

"Whatever reckless shit you on, my nigga, you need to chill," Tae said. "I'm cool wit' chu ready to get down on anybody, but you can't be doing no stupid shit and puttin' us all in a fucked-up spot."

Dro waved them off. "You niggas acting way too sensitive. Where that piece of blunt go? You niggas blowin' my high."

***

"Savages in the building!" the Hoe Whisperer called when Lunatic and Dro walked in the condo.

"What up, Unc?"

"Tell me somethin' good, Whisper? Did yo' boy ever call you back about J-Mac bitch-ass?" Dro asked.

"Nah. Nothing came up yet. He from Chicago, so he gotta be plugged with an organization. If he on count, we gon' find him. But first we gotta find out what deck he from. I holla'd at a couple board members. If he in the city, we gon' find him."

"Did you put enough on his head? Somebody gotta know where he at," Dro said, getting impatient. He wanted the nigga that killed his daughter dead two weeks ago.

"You gotta chill, Young Dro. I know that's hard right now, but you gotta get some discipline and control yo' anger and emotions. The police and the feds looking for the nigga, too. He shot seven people and killed two. You know they don't fuck around with a mass shooting. He laying real low. But something gon' turn up. Just give it time."

"I'm tired of waiting. I'ma fuck around and go to Chicago and look for the nigga myself."

"Chill, Dro. You way too aggressive, my nigga," Lunatic said. "You supposed to be done with this street shit, anyways. Focus on starting up them laundromats, nigga."

"I can't do shit 'til I find this bitch-ass nigga."

"Fall back and let the other shoe drop. Rushing shit is how niggas get fucked up."

"Shit easy for you to say, nigga. Yo' baby ain't laid up in the graveyard. Fuck everything until I get that bitch-ass nigga."

"I hear yo' pain, Young Dro," Whisper said. "Trust me, I do. But Luna is right. Don't let thinkin' 'bout that nigga consume you. We gon' get that bitch-nigga. Believe that. But you still gotta live yo' life. And you still gotta make money. How the fuck you gon' eat and pay yo' bills?"

Dro got up from the couch and walked toward the door. "I'ma holla at you niggas later."

***

From Whisper's condo, Dro drove aimlessly around the

city. He didn't have anywhere to go. It had been a little over a month since Asia died, and although he was healing physically, the mental, emotional, and spiritual scars remained unhealed. Festering.

He constantly thought of Asia. Sometimes his mind played tricks on him. He knew she was gone, but for brief moments he would say her name aloud and play out scenes in his mind like she was still alive. Emotionally, he only wanted to focus on the hatred for J-Mac. Nothing else mattered. He didn't want to smile, laugh, or play. Asia took his humorous side when she left. And spiritually, he didn't even want to think about God. Being a Christian and asking God for forgiveness of sins, or anything else, passed with Asia. The only thing he wanted was revenge. Relationships didn't matter. Money didn't matter. Nothing mattered except bringing pain on the nigga who killed his daughter.

Twenty minutes later he found himself in a familiar neighborhood. It had been a while since he'd seen The Body, and he decided to pay her a visit. Normally he showed courtesy by calling before he came over, but today he wasn't feeling courteous.

After climbing from the Charger, he knocked in the door and waited. "Who is it?" she called from behind the door.

"Dro."

When the door opened, Porscha stood wearing a yellow sundress and white sandals. Surprise and confusion shown on her face. "Hey, Dro. What's going on? It's been a minute."

"I know," he said flatly. "Can I come in, or do you got company?"

She noticed his downtrodden demeanor. "Yeah. Come in. You good? Why didn't you call me and tell me you were coming over?"

"I was in yo' hood and thought I'd stop by to see you. I

can still do that, right?" he asked, sitting on the couch.

"Yeah. But I don't like people just popping up by my house. What's going on with you? You seem… different."

"Lotta shit happened since I last seen you. But I don't feel like reliving that shit. I came to see you so I escape all that shit."

Porscha searched his eyes, sensing the darkness hovering around him. "Damn, Dro. What happened, baby? You seem so angry. Did somebody die? Are you in trouble?"

Instead of answering, he leaned over and began kissing her roughly, grabbing her titties.

"Whoa! Wait a minute," she resisted, trying to push him away.

Dro became more aggressive, climbing on top of her and ripping the top of her dress, exposing her breasts.

"Wait, nigga! Stop!" she fought.

He paused, staying on top of her, looking down. "What? You know how we do."

"But not like this. Something wrong with you, man. Let me up. You scaring me."

He mugged the shit out of her as he got up and walked toward the door. "I'ma holla at you later."

"Dro, wait!" she called, chasing behind and catching up with him at the door, leaning against it, not letting him open it. "What's going on, Dro? Talk to me, nigga. Why you acting like this?"

He looked her in the eyes, allowing her to see the fullness of the rage in his soul. "Somebody killed my daughter and my cousin and shot me up."

Porscha's eyes grew wide like they were going to explode. "Oh, my God! I didn't know."

"I know. And I didn't wanna talk about it."

"Damn. I'm sorry, baby," she mourned, reaching out to

hug him.

"What chu sorry for? You didn't do nothing."

"Because you hurting. I don't wanna see you like this. Are you okay?"

"Do I look like I'm okay? When I kill the nigga that did that shit, then I'ma be okay."

Porscha looked uncomfortable. "Damn. I don't even know what to say."

"That's why I didn't wanna talk about it. I told you that."

"Okay. I'm sorry. We don't gotta talk about it. What do you want to do?"

"Let me finish ripping that dress off and gimme some pussy."

She looked uncomfortable again. "I can't right now. I'm on my period."

He looked disappointed. "A'ight. I'ma get outta here and holla at you later then."

She felt compelled to do something for him and grabbed him by the hand. "Wait, Dro. Don't leave like this. Come to my room."

Porscha worked her jaw on Dro's dick, giving some of the best head she'd ever given. He busted twice, barely acknowledging her skills. The sexual act was passionless on his part. All he wanted to do was get off, and after busting twice, he reached for his pants.

"What you doing?" Porscha frowned.

"I got something to do," he answered flatly.

"Aw, nigga, you on some bullshit. I ain't no jump-off, thot-ass bitch. You gon' get some head and bounce? For real?"

He slid into the jeans without even looking at her. "Yeah. I told you I had something to do."

"You know what, nigga? Don't even bother calling me no more. You so fucking disrespectful. Matter of fact, lose my number."

He left the house without another word, hopping in the Charger and speeding away. He was stopped at a red light when his phone began vibrating. Figuring it was Porscha trying to curse him out, he almost didn't answer. But when he looked at the screen and seen Forever's name, some kind of emotion overcame him. He hadn't seen or talked to her since the Savages kicked her out of the hospital room. They had so much to talk about.

"Hello?"

"You sound different."

"I feel different," he admitted.

Silence filled the line, but he knew she was still there. He could hear her crying.

"I can't believe you did me like this, Ruben. I never thought you would hurt me. I love you, and you hurt me."

Hearing the love and pain in her voice tugged at something in his heart. "I didn't mean to do this to you. I'm sorry I hurt you, but I gotta do what I gotta do."

"No, you don't. You don't have to do anything. God will take care of it. All we have to do is keep our faith."

"I don't wanna hear about God, Forever."

The phone went silent again.

"Why didn't you call me or come see me while we were in the hospital? And how could you let your friends kick me out of the room? I'm so mad at you that I don't even know what to do."

"I love you, Forever. You know I do. But I can't be with you right now. I'm in a bad spot, and I gotta figure my way out of this. And right now the only thing that's gon' help me is putting them niggas that did it in the dirt."

"But that's not the way, Ruben. I don't want you to get hurt or end up in prison. You have to let Go–"

"I gotta go, baby. I can't do this right now. I'ma call you back when I can talk some more."

"Wait, Ruben. Don't hang up. I need to tell you–"

The line went dead before she could complete her sentence. Forever stared down at the phone with tears in her eyes and grave concern on her heart.

Chapter 3

"See, nephew. You can't get this pimp thang down if ya women think you soft," Whisper explained, taking a puff of the blunt. "I'm not a killa or gunslinger like you and yo' boys, but my girls fear and revere me just as much as the niggas y'all terrorized and took shit from. And why is that? Because I set up a system of rewards and consequences. That's right. They do right, they get treated tight. They do wrong, I tax that ass. But not in a violent way like the gorilla pimps of old, although I will beat a bitch. This thang is all about psychology. Gettin' in a bitch head and fuckin' her mind. All bitches got something broken on the inside, from the ghetto hood rat all the way to the First Lady of the United States. The key is finding out what's broken and then you fix it or offer them a way to fix it. When you do that, it creates loyalty and dependency. They begin to need you."

"How do you figure that out? How you know what they need fixed?" Lunatic asked.

"All you gotta do is listen. A bitch will tell you everything you need to know about her. That's the thing about women. They in tune with who they are, what they feel, and what's wrong. Problem with most niggas is we don't ask the right questions or listen. Most niggas learn enough about a bitch to get the pussy. Figure out she like jewelry, buy her a necklace and get some pussy. Figure out she like shopping, buy her some shoes and get some pussy. But for pimps, we get deeper than that. We find out what is missing from her life. If it's adventure, take her to places she's never been. If it's money, show her the fine things of life. If it's love, show her that shit don't exist. Teach her that life is –"

The ringing of the phone interrupted the lesson in pimpology. After checking the screen, he put the schooling on hold. "Hold on, nephew. Let me get this. Big Snake, tell me something good, OG."

"Ho Whisperer! Everything is good on my end. What that pimp life be like?"

"You know, pimpin' ain't easy, but somebody gotta do it." he laughed. "Was you able to solve that problem for me?"

"Yeah, I was. Had to do a li'l bit of digging, but I came up with a address. It ain't cheap. I'ma need twenty for this. The nigga is a plugged thug. His uncle got a slot with the fo' co'na hustlas."

"Say no more. Let me know where to send it and I'ma get that bread to you. Text me the address."

"You got that. This his old girl's address. Yo' boys gon' have to get what they can from her."

"Don't even lean on that, old timer. They will figure it out. And just a word of advice: stay outta they way and keep anybody you care about outta the way, too. When they come, they bringing pain, and it's gon' be a lot of damage. J-Mac fucked with the wrong niggas this time."

"I'ma heed the warning, my nigga. You be safe up them ways. I'ma send you the text and account information as soon as I hang up."

***

"*Ruff, ruff, ruff! Ruff, ruff!*" Scooter barked, his head hanging out of the passenger window.

Dro took his eyes off the road, reaching over and rubbing the six-month-old puppy on the back. "Hey, man! What you barking at?"

The dog licked his hand before sticking his head out the window and continuing to bark.

"You crazy, nigga." Dro shook his head, letting the

puppy do his thing. He had taken Scooter home after he got out of the hospital. Even though him and America weren't talking, she sent him an angry text threatening to kill the dog if he didn't come get him. Knowing how much Asia loved the dog, he went and got him. And in some strange way, having the dog around was comforting. He felt connected to his daughter by the American Boxer puppy.

After parking the Charger, he grabbed Scooter's leash and climbed from the car. "C'mon, boy. Let's take a walk."

The dog leapt from the car, leading the way onto the sidewalk. They walked to the boarded-up and seemingly abandoned house, going to the back door.

"Uncle Crush! Come to the back door," Dro called. After waiting for a few moments, he tapped on the back window. "Crush! This Dro. Come holla at me!"

The door opened a few moments later and a brown-skinned man with an unkempt appearance appeared. "Ya uncle ain't here, Dro."

"Where he at? You know when he coming back?"

He laughed. "The fool went and got himself arrested."

"What?" Dro frowned. "When? What happened?"

"Dee said he went in McDonald's and started throwing a fit. Walked behind the counter and started throwing food and fighting with the workers."

Dro laughed. "Yeah, right. That don't even sound like my uncle. Stop bullshitting. Where Crush at?"

"I'm not playing with you, man. Crush is in jail. Happened a couple weeks ago, right after the last time he seen you."

Dro gave the drug abuser a long stare. After realizing he was telling the truth, Dro climbed in the car and called the county jail.

"Milwaukee County Jail. How may I help you?" a

woman answered.

"I'm looking for my uncle, Christopher Patrick. I heard he got picked up a couple weeks ago. I wanna know if he got a bail."

"And you are?"

"Ruben Patrick. His nephew."

"One moment, sir. I'm looking him up now."

While the receptionist searched the computer, Dro thought about why the fuck Crush would tear up a McDonald's. He figured it had something to do with Savannah getting killed.

"Okay, we have a Christopher Patrick in the system. He has a two thousand dollar signature bond, but didn't sign it."

"What? He got a signature bond? Why didn't he sign it?"

"We don't have that information in our computer. The bond was offered almost two weeks ago."

"Okay. Uh, how do I get in contact with him for a visit?"

"Wait one moment while I transfer you to our visitation program. They will explain everything to you."

After listening to an automated system, he followed the instructions and made an account so he could reach out to Crush. As soon as he finished, he got a text from Whisper telling him to call.

"What up, pimping?"

"Young Dro! How you holding, youngin?"

"Same ol' shit, just a different day."

"I heard that. But I'm 'bout to make yo' day better. I got that information you was looking for. Got J-Mac momma address."

Some kind of darkness clouded Dro's features and his heartbeat increased. "Send that to me ASAP."

"Say no more. You be careful, you hear. He still on the run, but this should be able to –"

"Just send me the info, Whisperer," Dro cut him off. "I got it from here. Good looking out."

***

"Aye, Pop! Where you put the extra AA batteries?" Brean called up the stairs.

"They up here in the kitchen drawer!"

Brean climbed the basement stairs and walked into the kitchen. His mother was standing over the stove cooking yams, liver, and black-eyed peas. His father sat at the table going over retirement paperwork.

"Which one?" Brean asked, walking over and rumbling through the drawers.

"The one you in right now. I know you ain't blind, boy."

"He might be." His mother laughed. "He been smoking that K2. Know that stuff ain't supposed to be smoked. It's illegal."

"I found 'em. And you ain't funny, either, Ma. I ain't trynna get in trouble with my PO. Joe crazy. Ain't finna have me in Cook County on no bull."

"So, you'd rather destroy yo' mind smoking somethin' they made in a lab instead of just waiting 'til you get off parole next year?" his father asked.

When the doorbell rang, Brean grabbed the batteries and raced from the kitchen. "I got it."

"You know yo' son gon' go crazy smoking that mess?" Donna told her husband.

"The boy is grown. He gon' figure it out," George grunted, returning to the paperwork.

"Who is it?" Brean called as he neared the front door.

"Tray."

It was dark outside, so Brean clicked on the porch light as

he checked the peephole. There was a tall, brown-skinned man standing on the front porch. Things had been crazy since his brother, Jerion, shot seven people in Wisconsin. The police had searched the house twice, and he wasn't about to open the door for anybody he didn't know. "Who you looking for?"

"J-Mac sent me over here to give his momma some money," the man said.

That got Brean's attention, and he opened the door. "What you say yo' name was?"

"Tray," Dro smiled, going in his pocket. "I'm supposed give J-Mac moms some money."

"You can give it to me. I'll make sure she get it."

Dro pulled a wad of cash from his pocket. "Can I come in real quick?"

Thinking greedily, Brean opened the door. "Fa sho, my nigga."

As soon as he stepped foot in the house, Dro pulled the 9 mil from his waist and slapped Brean in the face. "Get on the ground, nigga! Who all in the house?"

Before Brean could answer, the rest of the Savages charged through the front door.

"Brean, you okay? Who at the door?" his father called from the kitchen.

"Who the fuck is that?" Tae asked, pointing a big chrome .357 Bulldog in Brean's face.

"That's my old man. Him and my old lady in the kitchen," he answered, holding his battered face.

Twenty and Tae ran to the kitchen.

"Who else in the house?" Dro demanded.

"Nobody. Just us."

There were screams from the kitchen before J-Mac's mother and father were escorted into the living room and shoved roughly on the couch. "What's going on? What do y'all want?" the father asked.

"Where J-Mac?" Dro asked.

"We don't know where he at. The police already come over here looking for him twice," the mother answered.

"We ain't the police," Dro mugged, "and we ain't leaving 'til y'all tell us where he at."

"We don't know where he at," Brean said from the floor.

Tae pointed the pistol at his father and squeezed the trigger.

Pop!

"Ah!" the old man screamed, grabbing his stomach.

"Somebody betta tell us somethin'," Tae demanded, pointing the hand cannon at the old man's head.

"Please, don't do this," the mother cried. "We don't know where he is. Brean, do you know where your brother is?"

"Nah. I-I don't know," Brean stuttered.

Dro slipped on a pair of leather gloves before walking into the kitchen and coming back with a carving knife. He walked up to the mother and pulled her aggressively to her feet, spinning her around and making her bend over. When she attempted to resist, he slapped her in the back of the head with the pistol.

"Get on yo' knees, bitch!"

After she knelt on the couch, he lifted the dress onto her back and sat the carving knife against her ass, pistol to her head. Then he looked at Brean. "You betta tell me where the fuck that nigga at or I'ma make you watch me fuck yo' momma with this knife and blow her shit off."

"Okay, brah! Okay!" Brean said, on the verge of tears. "He out west by Lasandra house."

"What's that address? And who the fuck is Lasandra?" Lunatic asked.

"She's one of the sistahs. I don't know the address, but it's the blue house in the middle of the block on Central and Madison. It's next to a white house with a wooden fence in the front yard. Just let my Momma an' 'em go. They don't got nothing to do with this."

Lunatic looked to Dro, wondering the next move. Dro shoved the knife deep into the older woman's ass and squeezed the trigger, shooting her in the head five times. Lunatic executed Brean and Tae finished off the father.

"You nasty as fuck, Dro," Twenty laughed as they walked out the front door.

"Move, nigga!" Tae screamed, pointing his pistol toward two people coming from a set of bushes on the side of the house.

"FBI! Drop the gun!" one of them yelled.

Tae's ,357 lit up the night.

Boom, boom, boom, boom!

One of the federal agents fell to the ground, a big hole in his forehead from a .357 round. The other agent returned fire while trying to duck for cover. Dro and Twenty clapped back at the fed, downing him next to his partner.

"Run, nigga! Run!" Lunatic called as the Savages booked it to the getaway car.

"Hurry up, nigga! Hurry up!" Twenty screamed, looking around for the feds' backup as Tae started the van and sped away.

"Damn, nigga. That was the FBI!" Lunatic panicked, looking around in all directions with wide eyes. "We just shot the feds!"

"They must've been watching the house," Dro surmised, also feeling nervous. Killing a federal agent was a whole 'notha ball game. One he didn't want to play in.

"Fuck that shit," Tae said as he whipped the stolen

minivan through traffic. "We gotta get the fuck outta Chicago. We burnt this bitch up."

"Nah," Dro spoke up. "We ain't leaving 'til we murk J-Mac bitch-ass."

"Fuck that bitch-ass nigga," Twenty said. "We just killed the feds, nigga. We gotta get the fuck outta here. Hit the highway, Tae."

"Shit, you think I ain't? We gone."

"Well, let me out," Dro said. "I'll find my own way back."

Lunatic and Twenty looked at him like he was crazy.

"You takin' this revenge shit too far, Dro. I know you wanna get back at that nigga but don't get locked up trynna do it. We gotta be smart," Lunatic said, trying to reason with his grief-stricken friend.

Dro reached for the sliding door and opened it. "Stop the mu'fuckin' van and let me out, Tae!"

"Don't stop this van," Twenty said.

"I ain't. Dro, calm yo' ass down. We gon' get that bitch another day," Tae said, making no indication he was stopping or slowing down.

Dro pointed his pistol at the back of Tae's head. "Stop the van, brah. I ain't bullshitting."

"Nigga, what the fuck you doin'?" Lunatic yelled.

"Chill the fuck out, Dro," Twenty added.

"Nigga, if you don't get that mu'fuckin' gun away from me, I'ma bust yo' ass!" Tae threatened.

Dro looked determined. "You gon' stop this van one way or another. Let me out or I'ma bust yo' shit, nigga. On my daughter, I'm not playin'."

Twenty seen the serious look in Dro's eyes. "Pull over, Tae. He for real, brah."

Tae pulled the van over and parked, reaching for his .357. "Fuck wrong wit' chu, pulling a pistol on me, nigga?" he barked.

"Ay, you niggas chill, fam!" Lunatic spoke up.

"I told you to let me out, nigga," Dro said flatly before getting out of the van.

"Pull alongside of him," Lunatic told Tae.

"Fuck that nigga. He just pulled a pistol on me. Nigga lucky I don't go open his shit up on the sidewalk," Tae vented.

Twenty climbed out and followed his nigga. "Dro, what the fuck you doin', nigga? Get back in the van."

He kept walking. "I'm going to get the nigga that killed my baby with or without y'all."

"You being reckless, brah. Get back in the van."

Dro kept walking.

Tae pulled up alongside Twenty. "Let that nigga go, brah. Get back in so we can get the fuck outta here."

"We can't leave him, dawg. We can't do our nigga like that."

"Shit, you 'bout to get left, too, if you don't getcho ass in."

"Y'all go 'head. I ain't leavin' my nigga."

"Stupid-ass shit," Tae cursed. "What you wanna do, Luna?"

He shook his head. "Twenty right. You know how we move. That nigga on some bullshit, but we can't leave him."

Tae laughed. "You niggas stupid as fuck. Y'all niggas get back in. Let's go take care of that shit so we can get the fuck outta this city."

Dro and Twenty got back in the van, and the Savages rode in silence until they were on Lasandra's block. After parking a couple of houses down, Tae spoke up.

"Dro, you ever pull a pistol on me again, nigga, you betta use it. I ain't letting you get away with that shit no more."

The goons had a short stare down, both men's eyes

promising violence if they were ever tested again.

"Say no more."

"You niggas chill," Lunatic intervened. "Let's talk about how we gon' get this pussy-nigga so we can get the fuck outta here."

"Straight up," Twenty agreed, checking out the house. "It's only one story. Let's look through the windows and see what we can see. If it look sweet, we can do a no-knock and kick the door in."

Just knowing J-Mac was close had Dro ready to kill. "Sound good to me. I'm with it."

The Savages climbed from the van, checking the block. It was dark and deserted, perfect for making a getaway after the kill. Dro and Lunatic walked to the front of the house. The living room was empty. Tae and Twenty went around back and were able to see a man and female in the kitchen. J-Mac was in the bedroom by himself. The Savages met at the back door to discuss a quick plan. Tae and Lunatic would shoot through the windows at the man and female in the kitchen. Dro and Tae were going to kick in the back door, rush in and kill J-Mac.

When everyone was ready and in position, Lunatic and Twenty started shooting.

Pop, pop, pop, pop, pop, pop, pop, pop!

Boom, boom, bloom, boom, boom, boom!

It took Dro and Tae two kicks to get the back door open. The man and woman were already on the floor bleeding, so they ran past them toward the room J-Mac was in. Dro got to the door first and was about to rush in when something in his gut told him to stop. Then he kicked the door open and let the 9 millimeter ride.

J-Mac was ready for them and wasn't going out without a fight. When he heard the shooting in the kitchen, he grabbed two Dracos and pointed them at the bedroom door. As soon as it was kicked open, he let the mini machine guns ride. Dro and Tae were barely able to get out of the way as high-powered rounds tore into the walls around them.

A moment later the Dracos went silent and glass broke. Dro snuck a peek into the room and found it empty. He ran to the broken window and seen J-Mac racing across the street. The 9 mill began sparking as Dro tried gunning him down. He missed and was about to jump out the window when Tae grabbed him. They fell to the floor as the Dracos erupted again. Pieces of the window frame and glass showered the Savages as they ducked from the chopper bullets.

When Dro looked up again, J-Mac was gone.

Chapter 4

"Crush, how you doing, man?" Dro asked.

They were having a phone visit. Crush looked like a new man. He had gained weight, looked clean, and gotten a haircut. Jail was doing him good.

"I'm okay, nephew. Waiting for the next court date so I can get the hell outta here."

"I called about a week ago and they said you had a signature bond. Why didn't you sign it?"

"Because I wanted to stay in here and clean up. Getting locked up was my way of going to rehab. I'm ready to change my life, and I didn't have the money for rehab, so I went in that McDonald's and acted a fool. I didn't hurt nobody really. Slapped a nigga and threw some food around. They thought I went crazy."

Dro nodded. "Damn, Unc. You a fool. But I hear you. You did what you had to do. When is the next court date? Do you need anything?"

"I don't need nothing. They gimme everything I need. Three meals and a place to sleep. I got court next week. Public pretender saying I should get a commitment or community service. Considering I already been in here thirty days, they might just let me go."

"I'ma be there, Unc. I hate to ask, but I gotta: is you done with that shit for real? I told you I would put you on yo' feet when you ready. You ready?"

He let out a long breath, tears watering his eyes. "You know as well as I do that when you lose a child, it changes you. I'm not doing this for me, Ruben. I'm doing it for Savannah. I'm doing it for Kathy, my only living child. Ever since I've been in here, I've been thinking on everything I regret. And you know what I regret the most?"

Dro thought about his own regret. "Not being able to save her when she died?"

"Yeah. I regret that, too. But what I regret the most is all the time I wasted doing nothing but getting high. I love my kids, nephew, but I didn't show them. I put my drug habit before everything and everybody. I want to try to make it up to Kathy. I'm tired of being sick and tired, nephew. I'm done with that shit."

"Okay. I got you, Unc. At least you got the chance to make it up to Kathy. Asia was all I had," Dro grieved, blinking away the tears that threatened to spill.

"I know losing Asia is a big loss, but you young enough to start another family and have more kids. Not to replace Asia, because she can't be replaced, but to restore some of your humanity and sanity. I can see you're harder and jaded. The light is gone from your eyes. I want revenge, too, but you can't let it consume you. I talked to the preacher a few times since I've been here. I still believe in Him. I got questions, but I still believe."

Dro let out a hiss. "I don't wanna hear that God shit."

Crush frowned. "What you mean, 'God shit'? You know I'm not religious, but God is real, nephew. Don't think for one minute He ain't."

Hot tears began spilling down Dro's face, burning his skin. "Well, if He real, how come He let my daughter die? She was innocent. Didn't deserve to die. Not like that."

Crush cried along with his closest family member, feeling his pain. "I can't answer that, nephew. I'm asking the same question. Preacher told me it's one of the mysteries of God. Mass shooting, natural disasters, famine, and disease. Nobody can answer why God allows it to happen."

"That ain't good enough for me, Unc. I ain't going. God is supposed to be good. He supposed to be love. Right now I don't feel no love. Ain't felt none since Asia died."

"That's 'cause you mad right now. And that's okay. I'm mad, too. And I want to get that nigga that took my baby. Do you know who he is?"

"Yeah. I tried, but he got away."

"That's okay. We'll figure it out when I get out. But in the meantime, try not to be consumed by the anger. That ain't good for you. You got anybody to talk to? What about Forever?"

Dro wiped the tears from his eyes and swallowed the lump in his throat. "We ain't talked that much since I got out the hospital. We not seeing eye-to-eye."

"Why not? I thought she was everything good that a woman represents. How you let her slip away?"

"Listen, Unc, I don't wanna talk about Forever just how you don't want to talk about Candice. Let's just leave that alone."

Crush nodded, understanding his position. "I'ma respect that. I just want you to take care of yourself."

"I am, Unc. Day-by-day. That's all I can do."

After the tele-visit with his uncle, Dro put the leash on Scooter and hopped in the Charger. The dog had an appointment with the veterinarian.

During the drive, he replayed some of his conversation with Crush. Unc was right about him being jaded. His outlook on the world had become dark, anger and aggression always present. Twenty pointed it out after he put the gun to Tae's head, and Dro knew without a doubt he would have killed his long-time friend if he hadn't stopped the van. A few months ago he would've never thought about killing one of his niggas. A couple days ago he was seconds away from actually doing it. He was dangerous to everyone around him, including himself. That wasn't a good thing, but he didn't know how to change it. Nor did he want to. The anger stopped him from feeling, numbing the emotions, turning him cold to everyone. Even Forever.

"Hi, Scooter! Hey, boy!" Karen, the veterinarian, greeted, letting the dog lick her on the face and lips. "He is getting so big. He looks healthy. What kind of food do you feed him?"

"I forget the brand, but it got all the good stuff in it. Iams, I think it's called," Dro answered.

"Yes, that is a good brand. Okay, I'll just do a quick checkup on him and then you can be on your way. C'mon, Scooter."

Dro followed Karen into the room and watched while she did a checkup on the dog. He tried to focus on the dog exam, but kept having thoughts about Forever. He missed everything about her. Her touch, smell, the sound of her voice, her laugh. There was no doubt in his mind that he loved her. If there was such a thing as a perfect girlfriend, Forever was it. And as much as he missed her, he couldn't make the call. Being with her made him soft, and right now he needed to be hard. He needed to catch J-Mac and avenge Asia's death. He couldn't do that with Forever in his life. She wanted him to let God handle the payback. Dro wasn't with that. Payback for Asia's death was for him to deal out, and him alone. So until he took care of the nigga that killed his baby, Forever and their relationship would have to be put on hold.

When Scooter was done with the checkup and given some doggy vitamins, they left the vet. Before heading home, he stopped at the grocery store to pick up a few items. On the way out somebody called his name.

"Dro!"

He spun around and seen a thick, light-skinned woman with low-cut blonde hair. She wore a white T-shirt, yellow leggings, and sandals. "What up, Shamika?"

"I thought that was you, nigga. What you doing up in here."

He looked at the bag of groceries in his hand. "I had to grab some shit for the crib."

She looked at him expectantly, wanting him to say more. He didn't.

"Oh. Okay. How you been since the funeral?"

Some kind of rage flashed in his eyes and he mugged her.

Shamika got nervous. "I'm sorry, I didn't mean it like that. I just wanted to know how you were doing."

"I'm a'ight. I gotta get to the car. Scooter in there by his self," he mumbled before spinning away.

"Wait, Dro! Hold on."

He spun to face her again, losing his patience. "What up, man?"

"I just wanted to, um, see if you thought about what me and America was saying about us all moving in together."

He raised an eyebrow. "You know me and America ain't talking, right?"

She grinned like she got caught with her hand in the cookie jar. "Yeah, I knew that. But I wasn't talking about her. She got her hands full with Block bitch-ass," she said, closing the distance between them, grabbing his free hand in hers. "I was talking about me and you."

He eyed her for a few moments. "What you on, Shamika?"

She smiled. "I'm trynna get on top of you again, nigga. What you mean?"

"You really wanna do America like that?"

"America not the same, Dro. She changed, and I feel like I don't even know that bitch no more. Like I said, she with Block bitch-ass, and he got her on some extra shit."

He frowned. "What that mean?"

"I'ma tell you while you driving me home. Where you parked at?"

"How you get here?"

"My cousin right over there." She pointed to a woman walking across the parking lot. "But when I seen you, I told her I was good. So, where you parked?"

He looked her over from head to toe, knowing he shouldn't be fucking his baby mamma's friend. But Shamika wasn't a regular chick. She was bad. And the thought of her big-ass booty bouncing up and down on his dick made him say 'fuck it.' "I'm right over here. C'mon."

Scooter was all over Shamika when they got in the car. "Hey, Scooter! Hey, baby boy," she cooed, playing with the dog as Dro drove.

"So, who is this nigga Block and what kinda shit he got my BM on?"

"Block a bitch-ass, dope fiend-ass nigga. Got my girl fucking with that boy. They over there getting high as the moon snorting that shit."

Dro looked surprised. "My baby mamma fucking with heroine?"

"Yeah, baby. When Asia died, that shit fucked her up, and I think she started fucking with that shit to block the pain. But now she just fucked up."

Dro contemplated driving to her house and beating America and Block's ass. But he didn't. Whatever they had was done. She was on her own. He kept on driving toward Shamika's house, thinking 'bout getting behind her phatty.

"I didn't mean to make you feel some type of way. Let me make it better," she smiled, reaching over and unzipping his jeans. Shamika swallowed his soft dick, quickly getting him hard and going to work. She sucked her jaws tight, moving her lips slowly up and down the length of him, taking her time and showing off her dick sucking skills.

The head was so good Dro found himself wanting to close his eyes and get lost in the zone. But he couldn't. He was driving. Instead he focused on getting to her house without crashing.

When he parked, she tried to sit up. Dro pushed her head back down. "Nah, go 'head and finish that."

She grabbed his hand. "Wait. Come in the house so we can do it right."

He cut the car off and took the keys from the ignition. Then his phone rang. It was Lunatic. "What up, nigga?"

"Where you at?" he panicked.

Not wanting to tell him he was about to fuck his baby mama's friend, he answered vaguely. "I'm out and about. What up?"

"You gotta come over to the condo right now. Shit serious."

He held onto scooter's leash, watching Shamika's ass bounce up the stairs ahead of him. He couldn't leave now. "I'm on something right now. I'ma shoot through when I'm done."

"Trust me in this, brah. You gotta get over here right now. It's serious, and I don't wanna say nothin' on the phone. Tae and Twenty already here."

"Is that Dro?" Tae yelled in the background. "Lemme see the phone. Dro?"

"Yeah. What up?"

"Man, bring yo' soft ass over here right now, nigga. We gotta holla."

Dro got mad. "Fuck you think you talking to like that, nigga? Betta watch yo' mouth 'fore I put blood in yo' shit again."

Tae turned up even more. "Come say that shit to my face,

square-ass nigga! You need to getcho ass beat, anyways. Got us all fucked in the game, ol' stupid-ass nigga."

Dro hung up the phone and spun toward the Charger. He was about to beat Tae's ass.

"Wait, Dro! Where you going?" Shamika called behind him.

"I gotta go take care of somethin'. I'ma get with you later."

***

After parking behind the condo, Dro grabbed Scooter's leash and walked quickly into the building. He didn't even bother waiting for the elevator. He ran up the stairs with the puppy and banged on Whisper's door like he was the police.

When Prianka answered, he forced his way into the house. Tae, Lunatic, Twenty, and Whisper sat around the living room. Tae could see the fire in Dro's eyes and tried to stand.

Before he could get to his feet, Dro tore into his ass, flooding the OG with punches in bunches. Tae grabbed him to stop the onslaught, and the goons began wrestling.

Not wanting to leave his owner on stuck, Scooter joined the action and bit Tae on the leg.

"Ah, shit!"

Twenty jumped in to break up the fight. "You niggas chill!"

"Break this shit up!" Lunatic yelled, getting in the mix.

"Fuck you niggas doin'?" Whisper yelled. "Them couch pillows cost fifty thousand! Ain't no fighting in here, and y'all bet' not get blood on my shit!"

"Fuck that nigga!" Dro spat, allowing Lunatic pull him back.

"Bitch-ass nigga, I'm killin' you!" Tae screamed, trying

to get away from Twenty. During the struggle, a black Glock .40 slipped from his pants.

"Chill, Tae. That's shit over with," Twenty struggled.

"On my momma, it ain't! Bitch-ass nigga gon' get it," he mugged, lip dripping blood.

Whisper picked up Tae's pistol. "If y'all gon' fight again, take that shit outside."

Tae realized the fight was over and calmed down, mugging Dro. "I'm done fighting. Let me go. Next time I see you, nigga, you betta be strapped. Gimme my shit, Whisper."

Dro reached for the 9 mil on his waist. "You ain't said shit, nigga. I got my shit now."

Lunatic grabbed Dro's arm to keep him from pulling the pistol. "Chill, brah. We ain't on that. You tripping."

"Nah, Tae. I'm not giving this to you right now," the pimp said, putting the pistol on his waist. "I'll give it to you later. You still hot, and it ain't gon' be no shooting in my house. Have a seat so we can discuss this shit. And I don't appreciate you niggas disrespecting my house like this."

"I don't got shit to talk about. Fuck that nigga. I'm leaving. Gimme my shit."

"Nah, youngin'. Go 'head and leave and calm yo'self down. It'll be here whenever you ready to come get it."

"C'mon, Tae. Chill, brah," Lunatic said. "We gotta holla 'bout this shit. We can't let this shit beak up the squad. We niggas."

"Straight-up," Twenty added. "We been through too much to let something come between us."

Tae ignored their words and walked to the door. "I'm good, brah. I said what I had to say. It's that nigga fault we in all the bullshit we in. Don't holla at me. Holla at that nigga," he said before leaving.

"Damn, Dro! Fuck wrong wit' chu, nigga?" Twenty

snapped.

"Fuck that nigga. Nigga ain't finna be talkin' to me like that. I already told that nigga 'bout that shit. Now he talkin' 'bout killin' me. That shit ain't just pop up. He been feelin' like that."

"Damn, brah. You niggas ain't finna be on that bullshit. Y'all gon' have to work it out. Ain't finna be clapping at each other over this bullshit."

"Shit, if the police find out who y'all is, y'all won't have to worry 'bout shooting each other. Y'all gon' be too busy trynna stay out them prison cells," Whisper said.

That got Dro's attention. "Fuck you talkin' 'bout, pimpin'?"

Lunatic answered. "Police asking about us."

Fear stabbed Dro in the heart. "For clapping them feds up in the city?"

"Say what now?" Whisper choked.

"We had to get down on some feds watching J-Mac momma house," Twenty said.

Whispers eyes grew as wide as golf balls. "Why didn't you tell me this shit, Lunatic?"

The tall, pretty-boy thug shrugged his shoulders. "I don't know. Wasn't nothing you could do about it. Plus, we in a whole 'notha city."

Whisper blew his wig. "Them is the feds, nigga! They got unlimited reach. It don't matter that you in anotha city. *Them is the feds, nigga!*"

None of the Savages knew what to say, so they kept quiet until Dro spoke up. "If it ain't about that shit, then what the fuck you niggas talking about?"

"Monster's daughters," Twenty said. "They must've heard us talking, because the police asking about me, you, and Tae."

Dro closed his eyes, feeling like the world around him was being set on fire. "Damn, brah. How we know the girls said our names? What if it's some niggas snitching?"

"You told somebody we hit that nigga?" Lunatic asked.

"Hell nah," Dro mugged.

"I didn't."

"Me either," Twenty said. "And Tae said the same shit. Plus, they didn't say nothing about Lunatic. If a nigga said it was the Savages, they would be looking for him, too."

"Damn," Dro mumbled, wondering how this could've happened. He should've killed the girls.

"From what I heard, they don't know who y'all is," Whisper spoke up. "They asking around in the streets and trynna put faces with the names."

"How you know all this?" Dro asked.

The pimp gave Dro a 'you gotta be kidding me' look. "Nigga, I know everythang that goes on in this city. I got people in important places. That's how you stay ahead, youngin'. The news don't even know this shit. Sensitive information. You niggas hot right now, so y'all might wanna stay off the street."

Dro looked at Twenty, regret in his eyes. "My bad, fam. I shoulda killed them girls, but —"

"Fuck that shit, Dro. No sense in crying over spilled milk. I ain't goin' out like no bitch. Them fags gon' have to come get me."

J-Blunt

Chapter 5

Dro lay in bed, staring up at the ceiling, unable to sleep. He'd been awake all night thinking about Monster's daughters. Quadruple homicide charges flew around in his head like vultures circling the carcass of dead animals. He should've killed the kids. But he couldn't. It was against everything he believed in and stood for. And that decision had cost him a relationship with Tae, and maybe now he was facing the rest of his life in prison. Damn.

When it rained, it poured. He was losing everything he cared about. Asia, America, Forever, Tae, his faith, and maybe his freedom. Pastor McClain's voice popped into his head. "If you continue to ignore God, He will remove the hedge of protection and the devil will have his way." The devil was having his way, and Dro couldn't understand why. Before Asia died, he had committed his life to God and changed his ways. Nothing made sense anymore. Left seemed like it was right and down seemed like it was up. The confusion made him angrier. He needed answers, but didn't know how to get them.

Then Forever's face popped into his head. Before he could talk himself out of calling, he reached out. Not wanting to wake Shamika, he stepped in the living room before Forever answered.

"Why are you calling so late?" she asked, sounding asleep.

"I wanted to talk."

There was concern in her voice. "What's going on? Are you okay?"

"Nah. I feel crazy. Ain't nothing making sense no more."

"What happened?"

"I can't figure out why I'm losing everything I love. I lost my baby, me and America ain't talking, I got into it with my nigga today, I lost my faith in God, and I lost you. And I might even lose my freedom. I can't figure out why all this fucked up shit is happening to me."

"You didn't lose me, Ruben," she cried. "I'm still here. I lost you. You're not the same."

He didn't know what to say to that. She was right. He changed.

"And why are you talking about, losing your freedom? What did you do?"

"It's something old. When I got shot before we flew to North Dakota? That came out. Me and Tae fought over it, and he said he gon' kill me. I know he ain't playing, either."

"So, what are you going to do about it? I thought you grew up together."

"We did. But it's different when it comes to throwing punches. When it gets that serious, you become enemies."

"What are you going to do about it?"

"I'm not about to let him kill me."

There was a pause as the fullness of his words set in.

"I don't know why all this is happening to you, but I've been praying for you. Do you remember the story of Job?"

He let out a short, irritated breath. "C'mon, Forever. We not about to talk about this God and Bible shit."

"You're the one who called me. If you want to talk, listen to what I have to say. You woke me up at two o'clock in the morning." When he didn't respond, she kept going. "Job lost everything. His house, his kids, his money, everything. The devil even made him sick with a disease. Even his friends turned on him. But you know what Job didn't do? Lose his faith. Everything around him was messed up, but he stayed faithful to God. And after Job prayed, God restored him, giving him twice as much as he lost. It's okay to be mad, but you can't lose your faith. God will take care of everything and give you way more than you lost, Ruben."

He wasn't able to answer.

"Ruben, do you hear me?"

"Yeah," he mumbled, clearing his throat. "It still don't make sense. Why would God let all this happen to me and Job if He loved us so much?"

"Baby, I can't answer that. Nobody can but God. And the only way you can talk to God is to pray. Have you prayed?"

"Nah."

"You want me to pray with you?"

He went quiet for a moment, not feeling the thought of praying. God had allowed all the bullshit to happen to him and around him. He was good on that.

"Ruben, do you want to pray?"

"Nah. I don't want to talk no more. I'ma call you in the morning. Go back to sleep."

"Wait. What are you about to do?" she asked, not wanting to let him go. They barely talked anymore, and she missed him.

"I'ma try to go to sleep. I got a lot on my mind and I need to try to make sense of all this shit."

"Okay. Will you call me tomorrow?"

"I don't know. But what did you want to tell me the last time we talked? Right before I hung up, you said you had to tell me something."

"Oh, um, I-I don't know. What are you talking about?" she stuttered.

"You know you a bad liar, right?"

"I'm not lying. I don't know what you're talking about."

"A'ight. I'm about to hang up. Go to sleep."

"Okay. Goodnight."

After hanging up the phone, he sat on the couch and

thought about what Forever said. He and Job had a lot in common. They both lost everything. Except the biblical patriarch didn't lose his faith, and because of that he was restored. Dro wasn't sure if he wanted to be restored. The only thing he wanted was J-Mac's brains knocked out of his head.

"Dro! Where you at?"

Shamika's voice pulled him from thoughts of murder. He got up from the couch and walked back to the bedroom. "I got a call and didn't want to wake you up," he mumbled, slipping into bed.

***

The dream seemed real. Forever was on her knees, sucking Dro's dick like she was a porn star. The eye contact had him in a trance as her pretty mouth moved smoothly up and down the length of him. Everything about her head game was perfect. She deep throated when she was supposed to, playing with his balls like she wanted to drain them in her mouth. His nut came quick, and that's when he realized he wasn't dreaming.

Dro opened his eyes and seen Shamika smiling up at him with her eyes. His dick spasmed in her mouth, spilling kids down her throat. "Damn," he mumbled.

"Good morning," she sang, crawling up his body placing kisses on his chest. "I don't know what time you like getting up, but it's 8:30, and I need my morning dick dose."

Dro grabbed handfuls of her ginormous ass cheeks, spreading them apart as she prepared to get hers. "Shit, don't let me stop you."

Shamika had some good-ass pussy. It was tight, warm, and slippery wet. And she knew how to fuck. She eased down on Dro's dick and rode him like a woman who fully understood her body, moving her hips in perfect rhythm, gyrating like she was using a hula hoop.

A few minutes later she spun around and rode him reverse cowgirl, bouncing her ass up and down like she did during a stripper show. The sight was mesmerizing, her enormous cakes rippling and jiggling. She kept at it until she got hers, then crawled on her knees, face down, ass up. Now fully awake, Dro climbed behind her and dove deep inside until his pelvis was glued against her big-ass booty. He wasted no time getting to work, lifting a leg so he could go deeper, long-stroking that pussy. Shamika's fingers slipped down to her clit, playing with herself as she threw it back at him. Their bodies moved in perfect rhythm, him matching her pace. She loving the feel of his stroke.

It wasn't long before Shamika was moaning, another orgasm rocking her body. Her pussy clench was ruthless. Even though he wasn't ready to bust, when her pussy locked around Dro's dick, it was all she wrote. He released inside of her, feeling the energy drain from his body in the seed.

"Bet Forever don't fuck you like that," Shamika laughed, staying on her hands and knees, shaking her ass at him.

Dro lay back in bed, not finding the joke funny. "Don't bring up her name no more. You don't know her like that, and she don't got nothing to do with what we doing."

Shamika sat up, surprised by the assertiveness. "I wasn't saying it like that. I was just saying I like what we do."

"So do I. But I ain't bringing up Jeff. When you with me, don't worry about nobody else. Focus on me and I'ma focus on you."

She smiled a little, liking the admonishment. "You know what, Dro? You right. If I'm wrong, let me know it. I respect that in a nigga."

"That's the only way I know how to be. But let me ask you if you on birth control or something? We used all the rubbers last night, and I wasn't thinking about it while we was fucking."

She climbed out of bed and grabbed the blunt off the dresser, looking at him like he was crazy. "Hell yeah. I ain't finna have yo' baby or nobody else's. I'm twenty-four years old, and I ain't ready to be stuck raising no kids."

Her reaction was amusing. "I like the way you put that."

"I think we gon' get along good together. I shoulda been gave you some pussy, but I didn't wanna do my gurl like that," she said, lighting the blunt and taking a couple puffs. "I love morning highs."

"So do I."

"Do you got some extra towels? I need you to drop me off at home, but I want to take a shower first."

"Yeah. In the closet next to the bathroom," he said before grabbing the blunt. "I'ma get in there with you. I gotta be somewhere later this morning."

"What you doing later tonight? I leave the club at two in the morning, and I wanna fuck with you again."

"I'ma be here. Just call before you come."

She laughed. "I got you, baby. I don't believe in just popping up."

***

"Ruben! Hey, brotha, it's nice to meet you," Dave Reed smiled, extending a hand, holding a tablet in the other.

Dave was a short, light-skinned man in his forties. He had a salt-and-pepper afro and was clean-shaven. They met through Charles, the nigga Whisper had used to clean Dro's money. Since the young shooter didn't know the first thing about starting a business, Charles introduced him to Dave. For twenty-five hundred dollars, Dave was going to walk Dro through the process of opening the laundromats. They were meeting at one of the two sites.

"What up, Dave? So, this is it, huh?" he asked, looking at what used to be a deli.

"Yep. And it's in a good spot. Right in the middle of a strip mall. Good amount of traffic. Residential neighborhood is only a block away. Wanna take a look inside?" he asked, pulling a set of keys from his pocket.

"Hell yeah!"

The building was bare, just a cleaned-out open space.

"I'll call some people and have them make it operational. Put in some tables, chairs, and pipes for the machines. Might need to call some window guys and put in a few more windows. I have a one-year lease for the building at my car," he said before tapping the screen on the tablet. "Also, these are the units you want to buy. Washers and dryers. They're used, but you can get them for a good price. You can also rent them if you want. Since you have the money, I suggest you buy."

Dro took the tablet and checked out the merchandise. He didn't know much about washers and dryers. They looked to be in good condition, so he was cool with it.

"Look good to me, man. I'm ready to do this."

Dave smiled. "Okay. Let's go sign the lease and make this building yours."

"Hey, do you think you could find me an apartment? One that's already furnished? I need to find a place for my uncle."

Dave looked toward the ceiling. "There's an apartment upstairs. It's not furnished, but I could talk to the property owner and get it added to the lease. You wanna do that?"

***

Dro left the laundromat site feeling better than he had in a long time. Finally, he felt like things were going to be okay. The conversation he had with Forever came to mind. Job got twice as much as he had before. All he had to do was repent and keep the faith. Dro wasn't quite ready to commune with God, but he was starting to warm up to the thought of it.

After leaving the site, he drove over to his family's house. He didn't have anything to do, and he told Shanice he would drop her off two hundred dollars.

"Hey, Rupaul," Kailah smiled, rushing over to give him a hug. Ever since Asia died, the family had been showing extra love.

"Hey, bugger bear. Where Shanice?"

"In her room. You came to give her some money? You brought me some, too, right?"

"What you need some money for? Ain't it 'bout time for you to get a job?"

"I'm getting a summer job at McDonald's. Daddy taking me to get a work permit when he get off work. But until then, I need a sponsor. Can I have a hundred dollars, sponsor?"

He pushed her playfully, going in his pocket and peeling off a hundred dollar bill. "I ain't nobody sponsor. Betta have Pops hurry up and take you to get that permit."

"Thank you, Rupee. Sometimes you a good big brother," she joked. "Now, come sit down and talk to your little sister. I wanna know how you been."

He sat down to chop it up with his kid sister. "I'm feeling good today. Most days I been like 'fuck it', but today been good. I met with somebody that's gon' help me open the laundromats."

"That's good. I'm happy you feeling better. You haven't

been the same, and I was worried about you. So, when are you going to start back talking to Forever?"

"I talked to her last night. She told me about the story of Job. We have a lot in common."

"I like her. Everybody do. And she's right. Job lost his kids, too. So, you getting back with her or what?"

"I don't know. She want me to do something I can't do."

"And what is that?"

"I can't tell you everything, but we not seeing eye-to-eye."

"Whatever you do, try to make it right with her. Don't let her get away. She is good for you."

"I know. I miss her. We'll see what happens."

Footsteps near the hallway made them look up. "Hey, Ruben," Shanice smiled.

"What up, li'l one?"

She reached down and hugged him before sticking her hand out. "You got my money?"

"It ain't yours yet. What's the magic words?" he asked, pulling the money from his pocket.

"Hurry up," she laughed.

He mugged her.

"I'm just playing, brother. Please. You know you my favorite brother."

He slapped the money into her palm. "I'm yo' only brother."

"I know. That's what I meant. So, do you wanna come to church with us on Sunday? Momma told me to ask you."

A coldness entered Dro's bones, making him stiffen. "Nah. I'ma be busy. I got something to do. Tell Momma I'ma have to take a rain check."

***

Scooter's bark pulled Dro's attention from the TV screen. It was almost midnight. He was sitting on the couch smoking, binge-watching Fifty Cent's show *Power*. And he wasn't expecting nobody until two o'clock when Shamika got off work. Scooter sniffed at the front door while Dro grabbed his 9 mil and checked out the blinds. There were no cars outside, and he didn't see anybody out front. Scooter began growling just as the doorbell rang.

"Who is it?" he called as he neared the door.

"Tae."

Hearing the voice stopped Dro in his tracks. Was this how it would go down between them? On the front porch? Just in case it popped off, he made sure not to stand directly in front of the door, in case Tae started shooting. When he clicked the lock and didn't hear shots, he relaxed, but only a little. After cracking the door, he took a peek outside before showing himself. Tae's hands looked empty. Dro kept his pistol out of sight.

"What up, nigga? Why you didn't call before you came over?"

"'Cause I need to holla at you. Let me in."

Dro eyed him for a moment, trying to guess his supposed-to-be brother's intent. Tae's eyes were hard, his face serious. Not a hint of peace in his energy.

"Yeah. Come in. Where you parked at?"

Scooter growled at Tae when he walked into the house, staying close to Dro.

"When you get a dog?"

"This was Asia dog."

"L'il nigga betta chill before I fuck you up," Tae warned. When he seen the pistol in Dro's hand, a look of surprise shown on his face. "I'm not on that, brah."

Dro locked the door. "I know. I had it in my hand when

you rung the doorbell. I didn't know who was out there. I was in here watching the last two seasons of Power. Come chill with me." Dro plopped down on the couch, sitting the pistol next to him. Scooter sat at his foot, watching Tae sit across from them.

"I ain't gon' lie, Dro. I been feeling some type of way ever since that shit at Whisper house. Plus, you upped on me when we was in Chicago. I wanted to take it all the way there with you. Had it been anybody else that did just one of those things to me, he woulda been laying in the streets bleeding. You know how I get down."

Dro's hand itched to pick up the pistol and blow a hole in Tae's face if he got on some bullshit. "I admit, I was on some extra shit in Chicago. I didn't wanna leave without making an attempt on that bitch-ass nigga, and you didn't wanna stop the van. That nigga killed my baby, and I wasn't gon' let nothing stop me from getting at him. With that shit at Whisper condo, I feel like you had that coming. You was talking slick as a mu'fucka on the phone. Trynna talk to me like I was a pussy-ass fuck-nigga. I got bodies under my belt, too. Based on the shit I did, I expect to be treated a certain way. Just like you want to be treated a certain way. When you went past what I thought was cool, I had to do something about that."

Tae nodded. "I hear you, li'l brah. Twenty and Lunatic said I was reckless with my mouth. I'm just one of them niggas that speak his mind. You know that. Shit, I been like that since we was li'l niggas. But I wanna put that shit behind us. You still my nigga. I don't wanna fall out over this shit. Twenty and Lunatic right. We been through too much to be on this bullshit."

Dro watched Tae intently. His mouth was saying one thing but his face said another. There was no sincerity in his eyes.

"I hear you, brah. My bad. I feel the same way. You niggas is my brothers. I know I'm on some extra shit right now, but y'all gotta understand I lost my shorty. That shit changed me."

"We noticed. And we feel yo' pain. You know niggas loved yo' shorty like she was our niece. Real shit. We all miss her, my nigga."

"I already know. But I'm trynna work through it."

"That's all you can do, my nigga. Just keep trying. Ay, you got some brews or something in this bitch? Something to drink?"

"Yeah. I just put a bottle of Rosé in there. Hold on."

Dro got up from the couch, walking toward the back of the house. He left the pistol on the couch, appearing unarmed. Before walking in the kitchen, he stopped off in his bedroom to grab the AR-15. Something in his gut told him Tae was on some bullshit, and he was about to blaze him if he tried anything.

Dro was standing in the closet, checking the safety on the chopper when motion in the mirror made him look up. Tae was walking into the bedroom, a black pistol in one hand, Dro's 9 mil in the other. They locked eyes in the mirror. Tae lifted the pistols and started squeezing the triggers.

Dro fell into the closet, barely dodging the gunfire as he lifted the AR and shot back. Tae ducked away just in time as high-powered rounds tore into the wall where his face had been.

He didn't realize Dro was strapped until the rifle bullets almost cut him in half. Not wanting to try his luck with two pistols against a chopper, he let off a couple more shots before getting the fuck out of the house.

Chapter 6

Dro moved slowly out of the closet, keeping the AR-15 ready. His ears listened intently, eyes wide, finger on the trigger as he searched the house for Tae. The front door was open, the frenemy gone. In his wake was another body.

Dro turned on the lights and seen Scooter lying on the floor, whimpering and shaking. Three gunshot wounds hit the pooch in the neck and chest. The sight was crushing. It was the last thing connecting him to his baby girl.

Tae had to die. He wished he had killed him as soon as he walked in the house. Any part of him that ever had love for Tae was gone. The Savage bond had been broken. His blood would be spilled.

After locking the door, he called Twenty.

"Damn, Dro," Twenty griped. "Fuck you callin' so late for?"

"That bitch-ass nigga just came in my house and tried to kill me!" he snapped.

That woke Twenty up. "Who? What the fuck happened?"

"Tae. I'm killin' that bitch-ass nigga," Dro breathed, pacing the living room with the AR-15.

Twenty couldn't believe what he heard. "Tae just came to yo' house and tried to kill you? On what?"

"He shot at me with my own pistol. I knew he was on some bullshit as soon as he walked through the door. Bitch-ass nigga killed my dog."

"Hold on, fam. I'm getting up right now. I'ma call Lunatic. We on our way. Just hold on 'til we get there, my nigga. I can't believe that shit just happened. Stay dangerous."

"I am. Savage."

Dro pocketed the phone, looking down at the puppy. Scooter had passed. He loved the little dog. They had bonded since he got home from the hospital. Not wanting to throw him in the garbage like a piece of trash, he decided to bury the little nigga in the backyard. But first he needed to get rid of the shell casings from the shootout in case a neighbor called the police.

He started toward the bedroom when there was a knock on the front door. "Hey, Ruben! It's Ronnie. You good in there?"

Dro sat the AR behind the door and opened it for the neighbor. "I'm good, Ronnie."

"I thought I heard shooting. My girl called the police and everything. You sure you good?" he asked, looking concerned.

Ronnie wasn't from the street. Him and his girl worked jobs and were raising three kids. When trouble happened, they did the right thing.

Dro knew he had to come up with a good lie. "Somebody tried to break in my house. Shot my dog."

"Damn, brotha! You know who did it?"

"Nah. I was 'sleep. I couldn't see his face. It was dark."

When the police cruiser pulled to a stop in front of the house, Dro's heart sank to the pit of his stomach. Two police got out of the car with flashlights shining, hands on the butts of their pistols. One was tall and black, the other short and Latino.

"Are you guys okay? We got a call of shots fired," the Latino one called.

Dro and Ronnie answered at the same time.

"Yeah, we good."

"No. Somebody –"

The policemen shared a quick glance, approaching the house. "Which is it? You guys okay or not?" the black cop asked.

74

Dro knew he had to make a decision. The cops were suspicious, and his response would determine if they were treated like suspects or citizens.

"Yeah, we okay. But there was shooting. Somebody tried to break in my house and shot my dog."

"Can we take a look?"

Dro didn't want to let the police in the house. The AR-15 was behind the door, and if they found it, he was probably going to jail. But if he resisted, shit would be worse. "Yeah. Come in."

"I'm Officer Vincent and this is Valdez. How did they get in?" he asked as they walked into the living room.

"I guess through the front door. I woke up when I heard the shooting."

"How many people came in?" Valdez asked as they flashed light upon Scooter.

"One, I guess."

"Did you get a look at him? Did you see the gun?"

"Nah, I didn't get to see him. It was dark. I didn't see the gun, either."

"Do you know what it sounded like? Neighbors said it sounded like rapid fire," Vincent said.

"That was my wife," Ronnie spoke up.

"Did you see anything?"

"No. We heard the shooting. About ten or fifteen shots."

"I'm gonna radio it in and see if we can get robbery to come. You don't mind if we look around for shell casings or bullets, do you?" Valdez asked.

At that moment, Dro realized he was about to go to jail. "Go 'head."

"I got shell casings in the hall. Look like nine millimeter," Vincent called out.

"I got holes in the wall," the partner called, following

them into the bedroom. "More shell casings too. Look like from a high-velocity rifle."

A few moments later Vincent walked out of the bedroom, looking at Dro suspiciously. "Looks like at least two weapons were fired. You own a gun, man?"

"Yeah. My AR-15 is behind the front door."

"Hey, Valdez. Come back up front. I think the story is about to change," Vincent called, looking behind the door and finding the rifle.

"That yours?" Valdez asked as his partner checked the gun. "You got papers?"

"I don't got no papers. Bought it off the streets."

Vincent reached for his handcuffs. "You got anything to add to the story you told us?"

***

In jail again, Dro thought as he sat on a thin-ass foam mattress inside the holding cell. Life was still whooping his ass. He was being held for possession of a firearm by a felon. He told Valdez and Vincent he was defending his house and planned on sticking with that statement all the way to the judge. Somebody killed his dog. He was a victim. The problem was detectives Jackson and Scott. They got wind he was in the shootout and held him for questioning, holding up the booking process. He had been waiting four hours.

"Yo' Ruben? You 'sleep?" Scott called outside the door.

When it opened, the detectives smiled like they were welcoming home a friend from a long prison bid. Scott stuck to his pseudo-street persona and wore designer clothes and jewelry. Jackson stood tall wearing casual clothes and running shoes.

"I wanna call my lawyer," Dro said.

Jackson smiled. "We got you, man. Come on to the other room and talk to us about where you got the gun."

"Y'all already know. I talked to Vincent an' 'em already."

"We don't know nothing about that," Scott said. "We only need a couple minutes. You'll get the call. Only way any of this will happen is if you come out the cell. But if you wanna stay in there, that's fine with me. It's up to you."

From the holding cell, he was led right into the interrogation room. The men sat around a small table, the detectives looking like lions ready to pounce.

"Tell us what happened at your house. Who killed your dog?"

Dro let out a breath. "C'mon, man. I already told Vincent. Somebody tried to break in. I need my phone call."

"How did they get in? What room were you in?" Jackson asked.

"I guess they came through the front door. I was in my room."

"Is the dog a guard dog? Does he bark?"

Dro seen the angle Jackson was taking. "Nah. He a puppy. Don't really bark that much."

He looked at Dro like he'd caught the Savage in a lie. "So, a stranger walks through the front door and your dog doesn't bark? How did you know somebody was in the house?"

"When they started shooting. I went to get my gun and shot back."

"Where did you get the gun from? Under the bed? In the closet?"

"It was in my closet."

"Was it loaded?"

"Yeah. Why keep a gun not loaded?"

"So, let me get this straight," Jackson asked, rubbing hands across his face. "A guy walks through your front door and kills your dog. You make it to the closet, grab your gun, and you have a shootout outside your bedroom door. Is this right?"

"Yeah. That's what happened."

"You know what I think?" Scott asked.

"What?"

"I think somebody tried to kill you. It wasn't no mu'fuckin' attempted break-in. It was an attempted murder. Nobody kills the dog if it don't bark. If the dog was a punk-ass mutt, all they had to do was kick its ass or give him something to eat. Somebody tried to kill you."

Dro shrugged. "I don't know about all that. All I know is somebody broke in my house and killed my dog."

"You Dro, Tae, or Twenty?" Jackson asked.

The question caught Dro off guard and he tried to act like he didn't hear it. "What you say?"

Jackson gave him a hard stare. "You heard what I said. Do I gotta spell this out for you? We missed the connection of you to the State Fair shooter, but we didn't miss this one. You connected to all of this. Monster. That drug house robbery started everything. Are you Dro, Tae, or Twenty?"

"I don't know what you talking about. I thought we was talking about who broke in my house."

"We don't give a fuck about that dog, li'l nigga," Scott laughed. "We know you killed Monster and his family. The daughters heard y'all names. We got yo' ass. That punk-ass dog should be the least of yo' concerns."

"I wanna call my lawyer," Dro said before going silent.

"We heard you say that back at the cell," Jackson said. "You'll get the call. But first, tell us about the murders. We know you were there. Work with us and help us. You cooperate and we will get you a deal. You don't have to go down for this. Why do ten when you can give it to a friend?

Why do life? That shit ain't right. Being a real street nigga is overrated. Ain't nobody in the streets real no more. It's about being free. Getting pussy. All the niggas that try to keep it real and don't tell end up doing life in prison. Don't end up being another one of the real niggas with life."

Dro held onto his fifth amendment right to remain silent.

"We about to do this not-talking shit again?" Scott breathed. "C'mon, Ruben. We gon' find out eventually. You gotta get out ahead of this thing. You and yo' boys don't got that much longer before we close the net. Don't be no fool. Betta tell us something before they beat you to it and all deals is off. Once we connect you to one of those names, it's a wrap."

Dro put his head down, refusing to look the cops in their eyes. He was keeping his mouth closed. "I wanna call my lawyer."

***

"What they say?" Dro asked from the passenger seat of Brandon's Lexus.

"You're a suspect in a quadruple homicide. Billy Carmen, A.K.A Monster, his wife, and two cousins. Apparently the daughters heard the killers talking and heard their names. They're connecting you because of the shooting a couple months ago when they said you dressed as police and robbed a drug house. Are you Tae, Dro, or Twenty?"

Dro knew if the police asked these questions, he was supposed to lie. But when the man you paid to defend you asked, he wasn't sure how to respond. On the other hand, Brandon had been referred by Whisper. Anybody dealing with the million-dollar pimp had to know something about street life.

"What if I am one of those names, hypothetically speaking?" Dro asked, not wanting to commit.

Brandon glanced over. "Well, hypothetically speaking, if you were one of those names, I need to know so I can begin building a defense. Actually, an alibi. This isn't my first homicide investigation, Ruben. I'm from Chicago. South side. Grew up in the middle of gang-banging. I did some myself, but didn't get too caught up in it. I know how it is in the streets. I became a lawyer to make money, number one, but also to help a childhood friend get out of prison. Unfortunately I couldn't get him out, but I put up a fight. I'm not one of those lawyers who will turn on a client. I knew what I was dealing with when I first hooked up with The Ho Whisperer, and I also know more crime means more money for me. Are you Dro, Tae, or Twenty?"

"I'm Dro."

Brandon didn't look surprised. "Okay. Is there anything that can connect you to Monster besides the name? Think long and hard about that."

Dro thought for a moment. They didn't leave anything behind and wore masks and gloves. And all the Savages knew not to talk about the dirt they did. "Not that I can think of."

"Okay. For now all we can do is wait. Is there anybody who can put you at the murder scene?"

"Yeah. Tae and Twenty."

"Do you think they will share this information for any reason?"

He and Tae were at war, but he was sure the goon wouldn't snitch. "Nah. My end is secure."

"Well, we just have to come up with an alibi. Do you have people that can cover for you on the night of the murder?"

Dro thought on his flight to North Dakota with Forever. "Actually, I had to catch an airplane that night. To North Dakota."

Brandon smiled. "That will help out. I'll look into it."

***

"Young Dro! What's up, playa?" The Ho Whisperer asked, dapping his fist.

"I don't know, man. I'm trynna get to the bottom of it. Where Lunatic?"

"In the bathroom. He told me what happened. That shit with you and Tae is real, huh?"

Dro plopped down on the couch. "Nigga came to my house and tried to kill me. Killed my dog."

"I heard about that. So, how you gonna handle that? You not gonna kill yo' nigga, is you?"

The look he gave told his heart's intent. "Hell yeah. He shot at me in my own house."

"Y'all gotta leave that shit alone," Luna said when he came around the corner. "We got bigger shit to worry 'bout."

"Fuck that shit, brah. He tried to kill me. Killed my dog. What would you do if a nigga tried to kill you? I just got outta jail. 'bout to be fighting a gun charge fuckin' with this nigga."

"I know, my nigga. Trust me. But we got other shit to deal with. That price on our heads is real. Nigga name Eddie putting that shit out there. We gotta all be together on this."

Dro looked at Whisper. The pimp nodded. "It's real. And they know who y'all is. I don't know how they know, but they do."

Dro shook his head. "Brah, this shit so fucked up. Twelve looking for us, too. Brandon just got me out. These bitch-ass detective Jackson and Scott the ones putting that shit out there about the li'l girls saying our names. I think it's only a matter of time before they put names to our faces. You know niggas don't stick to the code no more."

"What Brandon say?" Whisper asked.

"Come up with a alibi. I got a good one. I went outta town right after the move. I'ma go with that and say I left early."

"Y'all caused a lot of hell out here. It look like the reign came to an end. You know the sun don't shine forever," Whisper said. "Might not be a bad thing to hit town. Y'all way too hot in Milwaukee."

"I ain't leavin'," Dro said. "Not until I get J-Mac bitch-ass. You still ain't heard nothing?"

"Nah, not yet. But killing those feds made world news. You need to lay low. Stay outta sight."

"That's what I been doing 'til Tae bitch-ass pulled that shit. I need a pistol. Let me hold something, Luna. Tae took my shit. Where he at?"

"I got you on that burner, but we ain't gettin' involved in you and Tae shit. I talked to Twenty, and we want y'all to figure that shit out."

"Fuck that shit. I ain't got nothin' to say to that nigga. Let me get that banger so I can get the fuck outta here."

***

"Damn, nigga. You good? Why didn't you answer yo' phone?" Shamika asked after opening the front door.

"I just got outta jail," Dro breathed, walking in the house.

"What happened? You good?"

"Nah. I got a bitch-ass gun charge, and a nigga killed Scooter."

Her eyes grew wide. "Damn, Dro. What the fuck happened?"

"Some bullshit. I might need somewhere to stay for a couple days. Can I chill with you? I gotta figure out what the fuck going on. Nigga tried me at my house, and I ain't trynna lay my head there right now."

Some kind of a smile shown in her eyes. "Yeah. You can stay here as long as you need to. I fuck with you for real, nigga. I need some in-house dick. Do you know who did it?"

"Yeah. And I'ma get that nigga."

J-Blunt

Chapter 7

"Damn, my nigga. This shit crazy as fuck," Twenty said, blowing out a cloud of weed smoke. "Can't believe how the fuck all this shit turned out. We got the police on one side, prices on our heads on the other. And you and Tae clappin' at each other. Damn, Dro. This shit seem like it's too much. Shit seem like a Li'l Boosie song, my nigga."

"Where that nigga at, anyway? He ain't been home in a couple days."

"C'mon, Dro. You know I ain't gettin' in that shit. Y'all both my niggas, and I'm stayin' on the sideline. Unless y'all trynna holla and squash that shit. Other than that, I'ma fuck with both of y'all and try to keep y'all apart."

"This is why I wanted to get out this shit, brah. Too much bullshit. Niggas want us dead, and the feds trynna put us under the jail. Friends turned to enemies. Nigga took my daughter. If I was any less of a real nigga, I probably be dead. Another nigga in my shoes might've blew his brains out."

"You know that ain't no option for Savages. We thug it out. Niggas probably got that PTSD shit that them Army niggas be fucked up wit'. My cure is smoking, drinking, and gettin' pussy."

"Talk that shit, my nigga," Dro laughed.

"Speaking of pussy, what up wit' Shamika friends? Shorty got a phatty, and I need to see if she got a friend that got what she got."

"Me and Shamika ain't really putting what we doing out there like that. I'm staying wit' her 'til I figure some shit out. Her and America friends, and I don't think she want they mutual friends to know we fuckin'."

"You is a scumbag for fuckin' yo' BM friend. And not only that, you moved in with her. You a beast!" Twenty laughed.

"Shit happens."

"How that laundromat shit coming? I think I might need to look into starting my own business. I ain't been doing shit but spending."

"They doing the buildings right now. Should be done, like, next week. Then they gon' bring in the machines and shit. 'Bout two weeks from now it should be up and running. I need that shit to hurry up, 'cause I'm damn near broke. I only got a couple Gs. What you got? I might need a loan."

"Shit, I still got, like, fifty. Say what you need and I got you," he said before checking his phone. After reading the text, he looked uncomfortable.

"Who dat? You good?"

"Yeah. Wasn't shit. Lemme hit this bathroom real quick. I gotta make a move," Twenty said, setting the phone down and walking toward the back of the house.

Something about his reaction made Dro suspicious. He grabbed Twenty's phone, surprised it wasn't locked. The text was from Tae, telling him to come over so they could take care of some business. Just knowing the message was from his frenemy made Dro's body temperature rise. He sat the phone back down and plotted his next move.

"A'ight, Dro," Twenty said as he came back in the living room. "I'ma come fuck with you later. Put in a word for me wit' Shamika. Tell her I need a buddy."

"A'ight, my nigga. Stay dangerous."

"You know it. Savage."

When Twenty walked out the door, Dro waited until he got in the car before grabbing his keys and pistol and hopping in the rented black Nissan. He kept his distance, following Twenty, hoping to be led to Tae.

Fifteen minutes later Twenty parked in front of a blue-

and-green house on Milwaukee's West side. Dro parked down the block and watched. His boy got out and walk in the house. A few moments later he came back outside, followed by Tae.

Seeing the friend-turned-foe had Dro so mad he started shaking. If Twenty wasn't driving the car, he would've pulled alongside and knocked Tae off. Instead, he controlled himself. He got what he wanted. It was only a matter of time before Tae would be carried by six.

He was headed back to Shamika's when he got a call from the county jail. "What up, Crush?"

"Hey, Nephew. I just got back from court, and they about to release me. Can you come pick me up?"

"Hell yeah. I'm on my way. Why didn't you tell me you had court? I woulda been there."

"After you told me about the gun charge and being out on bail, I didn't think you wanted nothing else to do with courtrooms."

"C'mon, Unc. You know I woulda made an exception for you."

"I didn't want to put you through that. I'm good. Hey, you think you could pick me up something to wear? I came in those street clothes, and I ain't trynna stick my body back in those rags."

"You got it, Unc. I'm on my way."

***

Dro sat in the Nissan outside the jail, anxiously awaiting his uncle's release. He had already dropped off the change of clothes and was told Crush would be out within the hour. He couldn't wait to see the old man. Crush had been locked up for forty-five days. He couldn't remember the last time he'd seen Crush clean. It had been at least five years.

As he sat waiting for his uncle, Dro thought about all he'd been through since his uncle went in. His entire world had changed during those forty-five days, the biggest one being the frenemy, Tae. The world would be a much better place without him.

A few moments later Crush walked out of the building and began looking around. Dro wouldn't have recognized him if it wasn't for the T-shirt, Levis, and Nike Air Max he bought. He looked healthy. His hair was cut, face clean shaven, and he looked at least ten years younger.

"Crush!" he waved, tapping the car horn as he got out of the car.

The ex-drug addict smiled wide as he walked over. "Nephew! What's up, baby boy?"

Dro looked him over from head to toe. "You what's up, man. You looking good!"

Crush took a step back and struck a penitentiary pose. "You see me, Nephew! I'm dripping, baby," he laughed as the men shared a hug.

"C'mon, man. Get in the car. Where you wanna go? Wanna see yo' new apartment?"

He looked surprised. "I got a new apartment?"

"Yeah. And a job. I told you I was gon' hook you up once you got right. You did yo' part, and I did mine. Get in and let me show you the new bachelor pad."

"Wow, Nephew. You did me good, man. I'm lucky to have you," Crush said thankfully from the passenger seat.

"Nah, Crush. Don't even worry about that. We family."

"You said I got a job. How did you arrange that?"

"I got you an apartment upstairs from one of my laundromats. You gon' be the maintenance man of both properties. Apartment come with the job. You want it?"

"Stop playing, man. You know I want it. I don't know how I'ma repay you for all this."

"You don't owe me nothin', Unc. All I ask is that you stay clean. You owe that to yo'self and to the family. Just stay clean."

"I am, Nephew. I swear, I won't let you down. Now, tell me more about the nigga that killed my baby. Where he at?"

Darkness entered the celebratory atmosphere as Dro thought about J-Mac. "His name J-Mac. A Chicago nigga. We already killed his family. Momma, daddy, and brother. I had the drop on him, but he had some Dracos and damn near got me. But we got some eyes in the Windy City, and they gon' let us know when they find him again."

"I wanna be there. Matter fact, I wanna pull the trigger."

"I'ma take care of it, Unc. Don't even lean on it. I got it."

"The hell you do. That nigga killed my baby. I wanna get my gun dirty. Been a long time since I put in work, and I'm coming outta retirement. I want in, Nephew."

Dro nodded. "Say no more. You in."

"On a lighter note, how are things going with you? You didn't tell me who came to yo' house and shot the dog. What happened?"

"Tae tried to kill me."

Crush did a double take. "Tae? Yo' boy?"

"Yeah. So much shit happened while you was locked up, Unc. Monster's daughters heard our names and told the police. Whisper found out and told us. Tae called me talkin' shit, and I beat his ass. Then, about a week ago, nigga showed up at my house at, like, one in the morning talking 'bout he wanted to squash the shit. I knew he was on some bullshit and was ready. We had a shootout in my house, and he killed Scooter before getting out. My neighbors called the police, and I got arrested for felon possessing a firearm.

While I was waiting to see the judge, the same police that interrogated me for robbing Monster spot got at me again. They know the girls said my name, but they don't know who I am. Once they find out, I think they coming back."

"Damn, Nephew. This is bad. Why you ain't moved? Sounds like they closing in on you."

"Yeah. I thought about that. But I don't wanna run. I got a alibi. They don't got nothing but our names. Can't nobody put us in the house, and ain't no murder weapons."

"Wow. Man, I don't even know what to say. You got a lot on yo' plate."

"But that ain't all. Monster niggas got prices on our heads, too. And they supposed to know who we is. I think I'm more concerned about them than anything because we don't know who they is. That's how J-Mac got me. I wasn't ready."

"We gotta stick together from now on, Nephew. Wherever you go, I'm going. And I need a pistol. A six-shooter. I got yo' back. You've had my back for way too long, and I need to show my appreciation."

"If that's what you want, I'll get you some heat. Right now I'm focused on gettin' Tae bitch-ass. Nigga killed my dog. Used to be Asia's, and I felt like that was the only connection to my baby. I know where he been hiding at, and I'm going to watch the house tonight. See if I can find a way to get in."

"I told you I'm with you. I need a pistol. This time I want a revolver. I ain't gon' let what happened to yo' father happen to you. This time I'ma be ready."

***

"How you wanna play this?" Crush asked from the passenger seat of the rental car. It was after midnight and they were watching the house Tae was hiding in. They had been parked on the street for almost four hours.

"We just taking a look, see who he staying with. I never been to this house, and I don't know who all in there. I never seen the female that live there. I think it's just a li'l bird he shackin' up with because he know I'm lookin' for him."

"Okay. Been awhile since I was on a stakeout. You seem pretty good at this. You patient."

"Gotta be if you wanna do it right."

"Yeah, I hear you. Hey, whatever happened with you and Forever? You still don't want to talk about her?"

Dro looked over at his uncle. "Whatever happened with you and Aunty Candice? You still don't want to talk about her?"

Crush laughed. "Okay. I see."

They were silent for a couple moments.

"She asked about you."

"What you talking about?" Crush asked.

"Before the shooting started at the State Fair. Aunty Candice asked about you."

Crush smiled. "For real?"

"Yeah. Told me to tell you to get yourself together. I didn't tell you because you wasn't together, but now that you clean, I figure you needed to know."

The smile grew wider. "I thought about her and Kathy the whole time I was in jail. I need to see them. Try to mend those bridges, you know?"

"If you want, we could head over right now."

"Nah, it's too late. Plus, I ain't ready. We'll do it tomorrow or the next day. Gimme some time to get myself together. Maybe get a couple dollars so I don't show up empty-handed."

"Just say when and I'm there with you. And if you need

some money, I got you."

"I don't need no more help, Nephew. You did enough. I'ma figure out a way to get some pocket change. Don't forget, I'm a hustla, too. Been hustling back when you was in diapers," he cracked.

"Okay. You got that," Dro smiled. "I seen what I needed to see for tonight. I'm 'bout to call it a night. Go get some pussy. What you finna do?"

"Man, I would love to say I'm 'bout to go get some pussy, too."

Dro pulled out his phone. "You know what? I might be able to help you with that. You staying with me tonight."

After typing a text, they headed over to Shamika's house to end the night. When she got off work, she didn't come home alone. Her friend, Isis, came over and showed Crush a night he would never forget.

***

The next night, Dro and Crush were watching the house Tae was hiding in again.

"Hey, Nephew. I thought about a way to get a li'l money in my pockets to get me on my feet and give Candice and Kathy something."

"A'ight. What you come up with?"

"I need you to make a move with me. I got a vic. Nothing major, maybe a few grand. But that's all I need."

"You wanna jack a nigga?" Dro laughed.

"Yeah. Nigga treated me wrong when I was in the streets, and I can't think of a better way to pay his ass back than to take all his shit."

"Just say when. I'm looking forward to seeing how you put in work."

"You can see that soon. I thought about Tae this morning. I think we got what we need to make the move. That girl came back at the same time both nights. She obviously work second shift. Tomorrow night we should sit in those bushes and take her when she get home."

***

Tae sat in the recliner, smoking a blunt and watching his favorite movie of all time, Men*ace to Society*. He loved O'Dog. The trigger-happy youngster reminded Tae of himself when he was a teenager. He terrorized the city in real life, much like O'Dog did in the movie. Looking for someone to shoot for no other reason than he got a new gun and wanted to test it out was a thrill during his adolescent years. That was before the Savages had all their issues. Before the police knew his name. Before there was a price on his head.

And before he tried to kill Dro.

Of all the things he had done in life, he regretted what happened between him and Dro the most. Not the fights or the shootout. What he regretted the most was not killing him. Although Dro was the most level-headed Savage, Tae knew he fucked up by not completing the hit. And he knew Dro was out there searching for him just like Tae had looked for him. Dro hadn't been home since the attempt, and somehow he would have to track him down and push his shit back. That was the only way he would be able to rest a little easier. He needed to convince Twenty or Lunatic to pick a side.

A key being inserted into the lock on the front door pulled him from the movie and murderous thoughts. He reached for the Glock on the couch, making sure the safety was off. Even though he knew that was Evelyn coming home from work, he made sure to stay ready every time that front door opened. There were no rules in the streets laying down the law on how to kill a nigga, so he second-guessed everything and everyone.

He looked up as Evelyn walked in the house. The troubled look on her face made his instincts kick in. Something was wrong, and he learned a long time ago to shoot first and asks questions later. So he lifted the gun and started shooting.

The first three bullets hit Evelyn in the chest, knocking her backward. Dro held her dying body tight, using her as a shield while charging into the house. He couldn't get a good shot at Tae because he held the woman, so he fired wildly. Tae leapt from the couch, shooting toward the door as he ran to the back of the house. Crush was in the house as soon as Dro cleared the door, taking aim with the six-shot .357. Tae had almost cleared the living room when the revolver coughed once.

Boom!

"Ah!" Tae screamed as the bullet hit him in the back, knocking him into the wall and through a doorway.

Dro dropped the woman as he and Crush crept toward the back of the house. They could hear noise coming from the kitchen. Dro peeked around the corner. Tae struggled to hold his balance while trying to unlock the back door. Their eyes met at the same time, and they lifted weapons.

Pop, pop, pop!

Tae's injury made him a split second too slow. All three bullets from Dro's Smith and Wesson landed home. Tae fell to the ground, badly wounded.

"A'ight, Dro. You got me, nigga," Tae groaned.

Dro moved slowly toward Tae, keeping the gun ready, Crush at his side. "I know. But I wanna look you in yo' eyes."

"C'mon, li'l brah. Don't do me like this. We Savages,

nigga. Grew up and threw up together. Let's squash this shit. I was bogus for killing Scooter and shooting at you. My bad. We niggas."

Dro's face remained flat as he lifted the pistol to Tae's face. "God forgives. I don't."

Pop, pop, pop, pop, pop!

J-Blunt

Chapter 8

Loud knocking on the front door jarred Dro awake. He raced to throw on a pair of boxers and grabbed the pistol from the bedside table.

"Who the fuck beating on my door like that?" Shamika asked groggily, wiping sleep from her eyes.

"I don't know. Stay right here."

Crush came out of the guest bedroom half-dressed, the revolver in hand, a question in his eyes. "You expecting company, Nephew?"

"Nah," Dro mumbled as he walked to the front door. "Who dat?"

"Twenty! Open the door, nigga!"

Dro could hear the pain in his nigga's voice from behind the door. He found out about Tae. Not wanting to be a suspect, Dro prepared to get his acting on. Denzel Washington didn't have shit on him.

"Damn, nigga. Fuck you bangin' on the door like that for? I thought you was the police," Dro complained as he unlocked the door.

When it opened, Twenty and Lunatic stood on the porch looking pissed off and hurt. "What the fuck, Dro? You ain't have to do 'im like that, nigga," Twenty mugged.

Dro frowned. "Fuck you talkin' 'bout, nigga?"

"Quit bullshitting, nigga," Lunatic hissed.

Dro gave him the same confused look. "What the fuck is you niggas talking 'bout?"

Twenty and Lunatic eyed him suspiciously. Dro wore a poker face, watching them. Waiting.

"Tae gone," Lunatic finally said, pain in his voice and tears in his eyes.

Dro kept up the act, looking surprised. "Damn. Oh shit!

When it happen?"

"Last night," Twenty said. "Let us in, nigga."

Dro stepped aside, glancing up and down the street as he let his niggas in.

Crush stood off to the side, still holding the revolver. Lunatic noticed him first. "Crush? That's you, nigga?"

"Yeah. 'Sup, baby boy? Y'all had us nervous up in here, knocking on the door like that."

"Somebody killed Tae last night. Him and Dro been on some bullshit," Twenty said. "But you looking good, nigga. You look like you back right."

"I am. Sorry to hear 'bout Tae. I'ma go in the room so y'all can talk. You good, Nephew?"

"Yeah. Go 'head. Let me go put some pants on real quick."

"Who is that?" Shamika asked when Dro walked in the bedroom. She was wrapped up in the sheets, a little scared.

"Twenty and Lunatic."

She relaxed a little. "I thought them niggas was the police or somebody with a problem. Tell them niggas don't be knocking on my door like that. Why they ain't call first? What they want?"

He slipped into a pair of pants. "Somebody killed Tae last night."

"Who is Tae?"

"He used to be my nigga," he said, grabbing some weed and a blunt before leaving the room. When he walked back in the living room, Twenty and Lunatic watched him intently.

"On what you didn't off bro?" Twenty asked.

"Listen, my nigga. If I did that shit, I would say I did it. That nigga came to my house and tried to kill me. Killed my mu'fuckin' dog. I ain't do that shit. Y'all know niggas got prices on our heads. Had to be that shit."

"You way too calm, nigga," Lunatic said. "It's like you don't even care that our nigga got fucked up."

"On some real shit, I don't. That nigga got his issue. When he shot at me, all love was lost. I ain't fucked up about it at all."

Twenty shook his head. "Brah, that shit don't even sound right coming out yo' mouth. We grew up together, nigga. We Savage. Y'all had y'all issue, I understand that. But he dead now. Ain't no coming back from that. And you telling me you don't give no fuck? That's some bullshit."

"I don't know what to tell you, my nigga. It's one thing to throw some blows, but it's another to get into pistol play. I know y'all still love that nigga, but I don't."

***

"Pull up right here, Nephew. He should be coming out any moment," Crush said, looking toward the black-and-gray house.

Dro pulled on the side of the building across the street and put the rental car in park. "So, you wanna take what he got on him, or make him take us in the house?"

"Let's play it by ear. See how much he got."

A few moments later a tall, skinny nigga wearing dark clothes walked out of the gray-and-black house. Crush let down the window and waved him over.

"Crush, that you?" the man asked as he approached.

"Yeah, Chino. Get in the back."

"Damn, nigga. I ain't seen you in a minute. You all clean and shit. What you need?" he asked, climbing in the back seat.

Crush spun around and pointed the revolver in his face. "I need everything in yo' pockets."

Chino lifted his hands in the air. "C'mon, Crush. Chill. That shit ain't funny, nigga."

Crush looked at Dro and laughed. "He think I'm playin'."

Dro spun around and pointed the Smith and Wesson at their captive. "We ain't playin', nigga. Empty them pockets. You got a heat on you?" he asked, lifting Chino's shirt.

"Nah, man. This some ho-ass shit," he whined, pulling dope and money from his pocket and giving it to Crush.

"I know, ain't it? This for all the times you humiliated me, nigga. Had me begging you for a dub to get my day going. Knowing I'm spending all my money with you, and you treated me like shit. That was bad business. Let this be a lesson. How much is this?" he asked.

"Forty-five hunnit. And that's two grams of heroin."

"Good lookin', li'l nigga. Next time a nigga get down on they luck, don't be acting like a bitch-ass nigga. Get out."

"Hold on," Dro stopped him. "Give him that dope back."

Crush looked at him. "For what? This a hundred fifty dollars."

"Give it back, Unc. You don't need no temptation."

Crush nodded. "Yeah. You right. Here you go, kid. Thank my nephew for that. Now get the fuck outta here."

Chino pocketed the dope and climbed from the car.

Crush got his attention. "Chino!"

"Fuck you want, nigga?" he mugged.

Crush pointed the .357 at his stomach. "Take this with you."

Pop!

***

Crush stared out the passenger window, looking up at the house like it was a big-ass medieval castle instead of a two-story Victorian.

"You ready for this?" Dro asked, taking a glance at his uncle.

Crush let out a long breath. "I shot somebody the other night and robbed a nigga last night. But all of that seem easy compared to this."

Dro let out a chuckle. "It ain't that bad, man. Plus, I'ma be right there with you. You got this."

"It's been so long. I turned my back on them. It just seems weird. I don't feel worthy of their love or forgiveness."

"C'mon, Unc. Don't talk yo'self out of it. Let's go. You got this."

"Okay, man. Let's do this. How do I look?" he asked, brushing invisible lint from the front of his jeans.

"Like a million dollars, nigga. Let's go."

They climbed from the car and walked up to the house slowly, Crush leading the way. When they were on the porch, Dro rang the doorbell. It took a few moments for someone to answer.

"Who is it?" a woman called.

"It's Ruben," Dro said, looking to Crush. When his uncle didn't speak up, Dro gave him a nudge.

"And Chr-Christopher."

When the door opened, Candice's eyes threatened to pop out of her head. She stepped onto the porch, hand covering her mouth, momentarily speechless.

"H-hey, baby," Crush stuttered, about to cry.

"Christopher! I can't believe it's you!" Candice managed, looking him over from head to toe like he was a ghost come back from the dead.

"You look really good. How you been?"

"I'm good. C'mon in. Wow, Christopher. I can't believe it's really you. Hey, Ruben. How are you?" Candice smiled as she stepped aside to let them in.

"I'm good, Aunty. Taking it one day at a time."

"That's good, baby." After locking the door, she offered seats. "Sit down. Do y'all want something to drink?"

Dro had a flashback moment, recalling going with Forever to meet her father. "Yeah. Some juice or a soda."

"What about you, Chris? You still like those Crush sodas? You got Kathy drinking those things now. Got one in the fridge if you want it."

Crush smiled like he had just got three wishes from a genie. "Yeah. Pour me up. Thank you. The house looks the same. Is Kathy here?"

"No. She's in college. Stays down at the dorms around Marquette University. I'll tell you all about it when I get the drinks."

Crush wiped tears from his eyes when she walked away. "Don't tell her about this or I'll fuck you up," he threatened.

"You good, Crush. Matter fact, I don't know what you talking about."

He nodded. "Man, why didn't you tell me my daughter was in college?"

"I didn't know, Unc. I rarely talked to Kathy."

"I'm so proud of her," he said, taking a look around the living room. There were pictures in frames all around. When he seen the picture of Savannah in the casket, he couldn't hold the tears anymore.

"She looked so beautiful," Candice said when she walked in and seen him holding the picture. "Here are your drinks."

"Yeah, she do," Crush said, setting the picture down and wiping away tears. "I hate that I couldn't get myself together to see her before she passed. I shoulda been there."

"Nothing you could've done, Chris. God wanted his angel back," she said, wiping the tear that spilled down her face. "And you have another daughter you can be there for."

"Do you need anything? I got some money," Crush said, pulling four thousand dollars from his pocket and setting it on the table.

"No, I don't need anything. We're fine. Use it to get yourself together."

"Please, Candy. Just take it. Let me do something for you and Kathy. I need you to take this. I ain't gave y'all nothing in years. I need you to take this so I can know I did something. Take it for me. I don't need it. I'm good. Nephew been looking out for me. Just take it."

"Okay. Thank you. So, how are you? You look good. Are you clean now?"

"Yeah. Almost two months. When Ruben told me about Savannah, I knew I had to get my shit together. I need to be there for you and Kathy. I think it's important to let the people you love know you love them"

Candice looked touched by the heartfelt words. "Well, thank God something good came from her passing. Do you have a job? Where are you staying?"

"Yeah, I work for my nephew at his laundromats. And I got a little apartment. Nothing much, but it's what I need for now."

"That's good. I'm happy you're doing better. Me and the girls used to pray for you. God finally heard us," she beamed, staring at Crush like he was the handsomest man in the world. "Let me grab my phone and get a picture so I can text it to Kathy. She won't believe this."

While they were posing for the picture, Candice got a call on the phone. She gave a Crush a look before answering. "Hey, Billy. Can I call you right back? I have company right now."

Crush felt something tug at his heart when she said the

man's name.

"Yeah. It's the girls' father," she continued. "He just showed up with his nephew, and I was about to text a picture to Kathy." She paused to listen for a moment. "Okay, honey. I'll call you back as soon as I can. I love you, too. Bye-bye."

Dro looked at Crush's face during Candice's phone conversation and seen utter devastation. And he flinched when she told him she loved him.

"Who is Billy?" Crush asked, unable to hide the pain in his voice.

Candice noticed his reaction and felt sorry. "He's my boyfriend."

"And you love him, huh?"

Candice sighed, tears filling her eyes. "I waited for you, Chris, for a really long time. Two whole years. When I realized you weren't coming back, I moved on. I wanted to feel loved again. I'm sorry you had to find out like this."

Crush was quiet for a few moments, gathering himself. "It's okay. It's all my fault. I let that dope ruin our lives, and I'm sorry. I really am. I'm going to make it up to you and Kathy. I promise. As long as he makes you happy, I guess that's all that matters."

Watching the moment between Crush and the woman he loved made Dro think of Forever. He didn't know how he would react if she moved on.

"I do love Billy. He's a good man, and he treats me good. He'll do anything for me and Kathy."

"Then I can't be mad. C'mon. Let's take that picture so you can text it to Kathy."

***

After dropping his uncle off at the apartment, Dro sat

outside the laundromat and thought about Crush's reunion with the love of his life. It didn't go as planned. She had fallen in love with another man. Drugs had ruined his relationship with the best thing that had ever happened to him. That situation made Dro think of him and Forever. She was the best thing that ever happened to him, besides the birth of Asia. And he was letting her slip away. He missed her more than he cared to admit, and just thinking about her falling in love with another man made his chest burn. So he hit her on FaceTime.

"Hi, Ruben," she smiled.

When he seen her face, a warm feeling coursed through his body. Forever was beautiful, easily the prettiest woman he had ever met. Why she didn't become a model was unknown to him. "Hey. What you up to?"

"Wondering why you are calling me. We haven't talked in a while. Are you okay?"

"Yeah. I'm good. I been feeling better lately."

"You look and sound better. Like you're back to normal."

He smiled. "I've always been normal. What you talking about?"

"And you're smiling. I haven't seen that in a while."

"Yeah. I've been doing better. My laundromats about to open next week."

She beamed. "Oh my God! That's great. Is that why you called?"

"Nah, that ain't the only reason. I been missing you."

Forever melted. "Aw! I missed you, too. What is bringing on all of this?"

"My uncle and aunty. Crush got clean, and I took him to see Aunty Candice. Even though they not together, I seen so much love between them. It made me think about you."

"Wow. It sounds like you have a lot of emotions."

"I do. I don't wanna lose you, but I don't know how to stop wanting to kill the nigga that took my baby. I can't turn a cheek to that."

"I know it's not easy, baby. And I don't think it's supposed to be easy. This is a big thing. But just think about how God will bless you if you follow Him and obey Him. You don't have to do it. I don't want you to get in trouble. Think about me. You can stop it all right now and come over. I'm still here."

Dro went quiet, thinking on her words. He missed his girl like crazy. And even though he enjoyed the sex with Shamika, he didn't enjoy her presence as much as he did Forever's. But he couldn't drop J-Mac's murder. That nigga had to die. The sooner, the better.

"Ruben?"

He glanced down at the phone screen. Forever watched him intently. "Yeah?"

"Are you going to come over?"

"I'm not gon' lie to you, baby. I can't let it go. I can't let that nigga get away with killing my baby."

Chapter 9

"Whisper, what's good, pimpin'?" Dro said, dapping the pimp's outstretched fist as he stepped into the plush living room.

"You know you got it, baby boy," Whisper said before taking a drag from the blunt he was smoking.

"What up with you, nigga?" Luna asked before passing his blunt to Dro.

"Shit. Wanted to holla at Whisper and see if he got a line on J-Mac bitch-ass. That nigga still ain't turned up?"

"Still ain't heard nothin', Dro," the pimp said, blowing out a cloud of weed smoke. "Nigga hiding under a rock."

Dro plopped down on the mink pillow and took a puff of the high-grade weed. "Somethin' gotta shake, man. If I can't get that nigga, then I want his family members. Do he got kids?"

Whisper frowned. "I don't know. You don't feel like you did enough by killing his momma and daddy? You taking this revenge shit a little too far, ain't you?"

"I don't think I'm taking it far enough. Bitch-ass nigga killed my baby. I wanna murk the nigga whole family. Erase his entire bloodline," Dro fumed.

"You can't let this consume you like this, my nigga. Shit gon' make you reckless," Lunatic spoke up. "If you ain't kill Monster daughters, what makes you think you can do J-Mac kids?"

"Because that pussy-ass nigga killed mine. Whisper, I need you to call yo' man and see if J-Mac got kids. I bet that make his bitch-ass come out of hiding."

Whisper was silent for a moment, studying Dro. "I'm with Lunatic on this. Kids don't got nothing to do with this. I know you lost yo' daughter, but I think you going too far."

Dro mugged the pimp. "I don't think I'm going far enough. Call yo' guy. Find out if he got kids."

"I don't want nothing to do with this, Young Dro."

"Then gimme the number. I'll call him."

They had another stare down. "I can't just give you the number. But I'll make the call and let him know you wanna talk. Don't say nothing reckless on my phone, li'l nigga," Whisper warned before making the call. "Big Snake? How you doin'?"

"Whisper, what's good, brotha? How you been?"

"Good. Good. Listen, I wanted an update on that situation I asked you about. Did you get a location on that nigga?"

"Nah. He hibernating like a bear. Yo' boys came and spooked him. That fed shit got the city on fire. Fucking up everything."

"I told you they was gon' tear shit up."

"That was an understatement."

"I know. Check it out. One of my niggas wanna holla at you. He the reason we lookin' for O'boy. Here you go."

Dro took the phone and got right to business. "I need to know if he got kids."

"I don't know. But I can find out. Who am I speaking to?"

"This Dro."

"Okay, Dro. I'ma look into it and get back to Whisper. You know y'all got the city on fire, so anything I give you gon' come with a gas tax. I had to put out a lot of fires the last time y'all came to town."

"We don't gotta go through Whisper no more. I'ma give you my number. Put a price tag on it and I got you."

Snake's end of the phone went silent for a moment. "You know, normally I won't get in niggas' business, but I gotta ask. This shit seem too personal. Why?"

"I think you should stick to yo' rules and not ask

questions."

Snake chuckled. "That was good shit. I like you, Dro. I'ma get to the bottom of yo' situation and get back to you. And for that comment, I'ma set that sticker at thirty. You still wanna play?"

"This ain't no game, Snake. Get me that info and I'ma get you that bag."

After exchanging phone numbers, Dro ended the call and gave the phone back to Whisper. "I need yo' help."

"You know you got it, baby boy. What you need?"

"A way to get thirty racks. I spent what I had on my laundromats."

The Ho Whisperer smiled. "It just so happens that a fuck-boy fucked around and fucked in my bidness. Make sure you don't let the nigga live."

***

"What's up, Nephew?" Crush greeted when Dro walked in the apartment. He was chilling in the living room watching old gangster movies.

"I just came back from seeing Whisper. He put me up on a move. Supposed to be a couple hunnit thousand in the house."

Crush looked up from the TV. "Say what now? A couple hunnit thousand?"

"Yeah. Some pimp beef. Nigga tried to flex on Whisper or some shit. They had words, now Whisper want him out the way. We gotta go to Detroit to get him."

Crush got eyed him for a moment. "I thought you was done with the stick-up life. Thought that was why you opened the laundromats. Why you wanna do this?"

Dro took a seat. "'Cause I need thirty racks. That's what

it cost to get the info on J-Mac kids."

Crush's eyes grew wide. "Damn, Nephew. Not only is that an expensive price, but you sure you wanna start goin' after niggas' kids? I know you lost Asia, but this is a slippery slope you sliding down."

"I don't feel like I did enough to get back at that nigga for taking my baby. I don't think I'ma be satisfied until he gone. And since I can't get to him, somebody else gotta get it. He took my shorty, so I'ma take his. Ain't nobody in his family gettin' a pass as long as he hiding."

Crush let out a long sigh. "If this what you wanna do, I'm with it. Nothing won't bring our babies back, but I want some type of revenge, too. Let's get it."

***

Silky was more than a pimp. To him, calling someone a pimp was derogatory and disrespectful. He was of the mind that a pimp would do anything for money, even sell his own ass. Pimps worshipped money. Silky didn't. He worshipped himself. He was a god. It was a privilege for muthafuckas to be in his presence. In his world. He created his own rules and didn't believe in following the ways set by pimps of old. He made his own moves, and if people didn't like it, he didn't give a fuck.

Standing only five-foot-six and 150 pounds, he was a little nigga. His style of dress wasn't flashy clown suits like the pimps in movies. He preferred fitted, casual clothes and a nice pair of loafers.

"Listen, Carrissa. I told you the expectations of my ladies," Silky said, laying the rolled-up hundred dollar bill on the table next to the pile of cocaine. "I want real hoe bitches on the team that know they position. I don't wanna have to keep telling you what to do. You gotta know the role you play in the movie I'm making, baby."

Carrissa stood before him unashamedly butt-naked, following the house rules set in place by Silky. No women wore clothes when they stepped foot in his million-dollar mansion. "I know, my lord. But I wasn't sure how you wanted me to set this up, or how many girls you –"

"See, this is yo' muthafuckin' problem. You think everything and don't know shit!" the god-man snapped. "You need instructions on everything. You got so much potential, but keep gettin' in ya own way by overthinking every damn thing. How am I supposed to depend on you if you can't depend on yo'self. You don't even trust yo'self to make a decision because you so worried about making a mistake."

"I hear you, my lord. I just want to make you happy. I don't want to mess this up because I know how important this is for you."

Silky ignored her for a moment and took a big sniff from the pile of China White. "This is what I need you to do, baby." *Sniff, sniff.* "Take four girls and book a flight to Houston. I'ma have Meechee meet y'all at the airport. Go get that money. I'm putting you in control of everythang." *Sniff, sniff.* "If anything go wrong, it's on you. Can you handle that?" *Sniff, sniff.*

"Yes, my lord. May I be dismissed?"

"Yes, you may."

When the woman left the entertainment room, Silky turned up The Weeknd's song *I Can't Feel My Face* and continued to powder his nose. After getting higher than the moon and all the stars, he lay back on the couch and closed his eyes. The cocaine had his mind racing a million miles an hour. When the wind chimes sounded in his head, he laughed, knowing he was high as a mutherfucker.

A scream sounded somewhere in the background, followed by three pops. That's when Silky realized the wind chimes were from the doorbell, and the pops were shots being fired. He jumped up from the couch, accidentally kicking the table and spilling cocaine on the floor. That normally would've pissed him off, but he didn't have time to be worried about the dope. He needed to see who the fuck was in his house!

After grabbing the 10 millimeter from the table, he raced from the room. As soon as he stepped foot in the hall, a big-ass black revolver slapped him in the face. The impact sent him crashing to the ground as the 10 millimeter flew from his fist. His nose was shattered, and blood poured from his face onto the Tom Ford shirt.

"'Sup, pimpin'?" Crush smiled through the mask.

Dro, also wearing a mask, held Carrissa at gunpoint a few feet away. "Let us get that safe, nigga."

Silky took in the scene around him as blood dripped from his nose like a water faucet. Justice, his day-one, lay on the floor by the door. Blood pooled around the big man's head. That's when Silky realized he was going to die. So he stalled. "It ain't nothin' in here."

Dro blew the woman's brains out and let her fall on top of her pimp.

"Oh, shit! Oh, shit!" Silky screamed, shoving the dead woman aside.

"Got one more time to lie, and I'ma paint this hallway with yo' blood," Dro barked.

"Okay. Okay. A'ight. I got a li'l somethin' in the safe." The god-man trembled as he crawled to his knees and stood.

Crush grabbed him by the back of his collar. "Lead the way, fuck-boy, and don't try no bullshit."

"I won't. I won't. Listen, man. Y'all can have all this shit.

Money ain't no problem. Just don't kill me, man. Please, don't kill me."

"You good," Crush whispered. "We just had to make examples out them other muthafuckas. All we want is the money."

Silky led them to the master bedroom. There was a life-size painting on the wall of Silky wearing an all-white suit and a crown. Kneeling before him were twelve naked women, on their knees like they were praying to him. Behind the picture was a safe. After punching in five digits, the locks released and it opened. Inside was $175,000 in cash and some jewelry. There was also a chrome .38 Special with a diamond- and ruby-studded handle inside.

He went for the gun.

Pop!

Silky's body dropped to the ground like a puppet that had its strings clipped. Smoke wafted from the barrel of Crush's revolver. "Nigga was 'bout to try us, Nephew. Bitch-ass nigga."

***

It took Snake a week to call with the information. After giving Whisper thirty Gs to wire, Snake texted Dro the information. Turned out J-Mac did have a shorty. A daughter. And she was nine. Asia would have been nine later that year. It felt like some kind of twisted fate that their daughters were almost the same age.

And it was an even bigger waste that two children would die for something that had nothing to do with them.

Dro sat in the driver's seat of the stolen car, watching the mother and daughter walk down the block. They smiled, not having a care in the world as they headed toward the men who would shatter their lives. Crush and Dro had watched the family house for two days, learned the little girl's school release time, followed the mother to pick up the child. And now it was time.

"Let's do it," Dro said as he cocked the pistol and climbed from the car.

Crush followed, keeping the revolver concealed in his waist.

As soon as the mother and daughter seen the masked men, they stopped in their tracks, the mother pulling the daughter close.

Dro lifted the pistol, pointing it at the girl, applying pressure to the trigger. But he didn't shoot. He seen fear in the little girl's eyes and felt the same feelings as when he was supposed to kill Monster's daughters. Then Asia's face took the place of the little girl's, making Dro freeze. For a moment he thought he was really seeing his daughter.

Then the mother and daughter screamed, the noise clearing his mind and putting him back in the moment. When Crush seen his nephew freeze, he pulled his revolver and got down to business. He fired four shots into the mother's chest and face. The little girl wailed over her mother as they jumped in the car.

"What the fuck you freeze for? What happened, Nephew?" Crush asked, looking around in all directions as Dro sped away from the scene.

"I couldn't do it, Unc. I couldn't kill her. I seen Asia's face and I froze," He admitted.

"I knew you wasn't gon' do it. I couldn't do it, either. That's why I killed her mother. The girl will grow up to know what it feels like to have something taken from her. And J-Mac will know he caused his daughter's pain.

Chapter 10

Dro stood inside the laundromat, disappointment flooding his body. Today was the grand opening for his business ventures. Dave told him to taper his expectations because it would take a few months to garner community support and start making profits. The warning was an understatement. Six people showed up to wash clothes. Just six. He wanted to believe in Dave's words, that things would get greater later, but judging by the first day of business, it was hard to see it getting better.

"It'll get better, Nephew. This is just the first day," Crush spoke as he walked over to stand beside Dro.

"You read my mind, Unc. Six people showed up to wash. I was expecting more. Man, I hope I didn't waste my money."

Crush laughed. "I'ma give you some bad news followed by good news. Over fifty percent of businesses fail when they first open. But, there are some businesses that are fail-proof and recession-proof. A laundromat is one of those businesses."

Dro focused on the negative. "Fifty percent of businesses fail, huh?"

"You didn't hear what I said about fail-proof businesses?"

"Yeah. But it's hard to ignore the bad news. Especially after today."

"You'll be okay, Nephew. Plus, it's not like we broke. Still got that come-up from the pimp. I got fifty thousand. I've never had this much money before, and don't know what to do with it. If the laundromats go under, which I know they won't, we can try it again with something else."

Dro let out a breath. "Yeah, you right. I still got some money, too. Hey, I'ma go check on the other site. You wanna stay here or roll with me?"

"I told you that you ain't going nowhere without me. I'm riding. Let's do it."

They stepped outside, walking toward the rental car when an older man carrying a homemade sign walked up. The sign read 'THE END IS HERE'

"Repent and be baptized in the name of Jesus, young man! The time is almost here. The rapture is coming!"

Dro gave him a crazy look and tried to side-step him. "A'ight, man."

Instead of leaving them alone, he got bolder. "Don't ignore me, young man. Your soul is on the line. The life God put in you is larger than the life you're living. Come to God. The end is almost here."

The words made Dro pause. "What you just say?"

"Don't pay him no mind, Nephew. Get in the car," Crush intervened. "Move around, man."

The sidewalk evangelist locked eyes with Dro. "God is calling you, young man. Listen to him. Don't ignore the Lord. The life he put in you is larger than the life you've been living."

Crush walked over and gave the man a shove. "Okay, man. That's enough of that. Get outta here!"

He walked away, keeping eye contact with Dro. "God is alive! Listen to him! God is real!"

"It's some crazy muthafuckas out here," Crush laughed, climbing in the passenger seat of the rental car.

***

"You don't gotta work tonight?" Dro asked after using his key to let himself in Shamika's house.

She sat on the couch in sweatpants and a t-shirt watching *Love and Hip Hop*. "Nah. It's Tuesday. A slow night. But forget about me, how was the opening of the laundromats?"

Dro sunk down on the couch next to her. "Didn't hardly

nobody show up. I'm wondering if I wasted my money on these damn things."

"But it was only the first day. Was you really expecting a lot of people to show up? It wasn't like you was opening a store."

"I don't know what I was expecting. People been telling me the traffic will pick up in time. I guess I was just expecting more."

Shamika poked out her bottom lip, reaching over to give him a hug. "Aw. You sound sad."

"Nah, I ain't sad. I'm good. I just don't want to lose my fuckin' money. Some other crazy shit happened to me, too. One of them sidewalk preachers walked up and got to talking about 'God is real and is calling me.' Shit had me feeling some type of way."

Shamika laughed. "Them street preachers be crazy as fuck. I had one walk up to me and say God told him to tell me to give him a hundred dollars. I told his ass why the fuck God ain't tell me to give him the money. I don't believe all that shit them preachers be talking. I think they be pimps and scammers. What you think?"

"I think it's real. I believe in what them preachers be saying. I was raised up in church."

She looked surprised. "You used to be a church boy?"

"Something like that. I always felt like God was watching me and looking out for me. I know the shit sound crazy, but this real. Then the nigga said a quote that I heard a preacher say right before I got shot. Shit was crazy."

"Let me find out you was in the choir, nigga. Be catching the holy ghost and falling out in the church pews," she cracked.

"Fuck you," he laughed.

"Betta stop playin' with me, nigga. That shit sound like

foreplay," she said, reaching over and grabbing his dick through his pants.

"You betta stop playin' with me. Don't be grabbing this mu'fucka if you ain't gon' do nothing wit' it."

The playful moment was instantly changed to a sexual vibe. "You the one playin'. I'll put this pussy on yo' mustache and change yo' life, nigga. Say I won't."

Dro took the challenge, dropping his pistol on the floor and standing to undress. "Why you still talking? Show me."

Shamika stripped from the sweats and t-shirt before pushing him on the couch and climbing on top in the sixty-nine position. She took his dick in her mouth and went to work, head bobbing up and down rapidly. She sucked him hard, giving sloppy head, spit dripping down his balls. Dro moaned in pleasure, loving Shamika's head game. She was a champ. But she had also talked shit, and he had to put up or shut up.

Instead of shutting up, he opened his mouth and attacked her pearl tongue, sucking on it like it was a piece of candy. Feeling like he had to put on and make her bust first, he moved his hand to her pussy. She was so wet that two fingers slipped right in. He used his other hand to slip a finger in her ass.

Shamika got caught up in the moment, lifting her head to scream out in pleasure as he stimulated all of her holes.

"Oh shit, nigga! Hell, yeah! Eat that pussy!"

Dro continued to deliver maximum pleasure, thrusting his hips up and poking her chin with his dick.

Getting the message, Shamika slurped him back in her mouth and went to work. But she couldn't handle Dro's lips and fingers. She lifted her head again, screaming as a powerful orgasm racked her body.

"Oh my God! Oh shit! Ah!"

While she took a moment to catch her breath, Dro stood up, smiling, knowing he had won that round. "Open wide."

Shamika sat upright on the couch while he stood before her. When she was ready, he slipped his dick in her mouth, shoving it down her throat until her lips were touching his pelvis. Shamika gagged, but didn't back out. Dro began fucking her mouth like it was her pussy, grabbing the back of her head.

Shamika looked up at him, maintaining eye contact while he punished her tonsils. Shit was sexy as fuck and had Dro's nut coming quicker than he wanted. But instead of letting her swallow it, he pulled out and jacked off, releasing on her face.

"Oh yeah, baby," Shamika moaned, loving the feel of his dick painting cum on her face. "I love this nasty shit."

"Get on them knees," he told her, not even allowing her to a chance to clean her face.

Shamika spun around and knelt on the couch. Dro stood behind her and admired her big-ass booty before diving deep into her pussy. Her ass bounced and jiggled against his pelvis as he tore the pussy up.

"Oh shit, baby. Damn, Dro!" she moaned.

"Don't nobody fuck you like I do, do they?" he asked, slapping her big-ass booty and watching it ripple.

"Nah, baby. Oh shit. Don't nobody. Fuck. Ooh, yeah. Fuck me. Like. You," she managed.

He slapped her ass again. "This my pussy, ain't it? You love the way I fuck my pussy, don't you?"

"Ooh, yeah, Dro. This yo'. Oh shit. This yo' pussy, baby. This pussy. All yours."

Dro continued to wax her ass from behind, slapping them cheeks, and Shamika loved it. When he was ready to bust again, he pulled out and skeeted on her back.

"Damn, nigga. That shit was fire," Shamika smiled as she

stood up. "Now come fuck me in the shower and nut on me some more."

After another round of freaky-ass sex in the shower, Shamika cooked pork chops and macaroni and they chilled in front of the TV. They were watching *Power* when the doorbell rang.

Dro checked the time on his phone. It was eleven o'clock at night. "You expecting company?"

"Nah. They know to call first. Is it somebody for you?"

"Nah," Dro said, grabbing his pistol from the floor and standing on the side of the door. "Who is it?"

"America. Where Shamika?"

Shamika's eyes grew wide.

Dro's eyes grew wider. "Shit. How you wanna play this?"

She looked Dro over from head to toe. All he wore was boxers, and she wore his t-shirt. "I don't know. What you wanna do?"

He paused to think, not liking the thought of hiding from nobody, but he didn't want unnecessary drama.

"Shamika! Let me in, bitch!" America called, slapping the door.

He shrugged before going to sit on the couch and tucking the pistol under a pillow. "It's on you. We can handle this however you want."

Shamika looked scared and nervous as she opened the door enough to stick her head out. America stood on the porch looking sour. A short, dark-skinned nigga with nappy dreads stood on the porch with her.

"Hey, America. What you doing coming over this late? I'm kinda busy."

"I need to holla at you. Can I come in?"

"Um, I'm in the middle of something. Can it wait 'til tomorrow?"

America's face dropped in disappointment. "That's how you gon' do me? Gon' kick yo' friend to the curb for some dick? Just let me in real quick. It's important."

Shamika looked back at Dro.

"Um, America, I don't know how to tell you this but, um, Dro here. We been messing around."

America's face reflected a bunch of emotions – confusion, surprise, and anger. When it hit her that Dro answered the door, her face twisted up in a mug. "Oh, hell nah!" she said, pushing the door open.

Dro was sitting on the couch wearing a neutral look.

"This how y'all do me, for real?" America shrieked.

"Wait, America. It ain't like that."

She turned up the attitude. "What you mean, it ain't like that? Bitch, you fuckin' my baby daddy!"

"I know. But me and you stopped talking. It just happened. I wasn't trynna hurt you," Shamika pleaded.

America pushed past the backstabber and got in Dro's face. "Nigga, this how you do? Gon' fuck my friend behind my back!"

"Fuck out my face, America," Dro growled, keeping his voice under control.

"Fuck that shit, nigga. You fuckin' my friend," she yelled, muffing him in the face.

Dro had never put his hands on his baby mama. All that changed after she pushed him in the face. He jumped up, reaching a hand back, and slapping the shit out of America.

"Aye, nigga! Don't be hittin' her!" Block yelled, rushing into the house and pushing Dro.

The Savage's reaction was quick, a right cross connecting to Block's jaw. The smaller man stumbled backward, and Dro rushed him, swinging wild punches.

While the men fought, America attacked her ex-best

friend and the women got it on. The ladies didn't pull hair and scratch. They threw blows like they had been boxing all their lives. Nobody seemed to be winning or losing as America and Shamika threw down.

The men's fight was far more one-sided. Dro got the advantage and whooped Block's ass. When the smaller man realized he had no win, he ran out of the house. Dro moved over to pull Shamika and America apart.

"A'ight, y'all. Break this shit up. It's over."

"Punks-ass bitch!" Shamika yelled, pulling a patch of hair from America's head. "Gimme this weave."

"I don't give a fuck about that hair, bitch. You mu'fuckas bogus. How y'all gon' do me like that?"

"Leave this shit alone. We doin' us. You do you," Dro said.

"Nah, fuck that. You s'posed to be my friend, Shamika."

Shamika grabbed Dro's dick through his boxers. "Me and yo' baby daddy make better friends. Get the fuck outta my house, bitch. Go snort some more of that shit with yo' dope fiend-ass nigga."

America stood there for a moment, hurt and betrayal drawn on her face. "Both of y'all some bitch-ass niggas. Y'all gon' get it back. I promise."

Chapter 11

"How long you think it'll take us to get these niggas and get the fuck outta Wisconsin?" Cherry asked.

Dirty glanced around the coach section, watching the passengers getting ready to exit the airplane. They had just landed in Milwaukee's airport and were about to get off the plane as well. Except Dirty was taking his time.

"However long it take to get that bag. It's four of these niggas. That's two hunnit stickers. We gon' do what we can and then move on. Ain't no time limit on gettin' it."

"I just don't like it here. My friend Jazzy nigga came to Wisconsin a couple years ago trynna get some money. He got locked up and ain't came back home yet."

"That means we can't get knocked. I ain't going back to the bing. If the police get on our ass, I'm holding court wherever they run up on me at. I ain't playin'. Now, let's get the fuck off this plane. The longer it take us to get off, the longer it's gon' take us to get that bag."

After getting off the 747, they made their way through Mitchell International Airport, stopping at baggage claim to pick up their bags.

"Where yo' cousin?" Cherry asked, looking around.

Dirty was doing the same. "I don't see him. Lemme send him a text."

"Dirty!"

He spun around at the sound of his name and seen a chubby, light-skinned nigga walking over. The fat nigga was smiling from ear to ear, dressed in snug-fitting designer clothes, his short afro uncombed.

"Eddie? Damn, you got fat as a muthafucka, nigga!" Dirty smiled, reaching out to hug his cousin.

The big man rubbed his stomach. "Nigga was out here

eatin'. I see you was in there gettin' to them weights. Niggas ain't on that shit. You don't need muscles when you got money."

"And you don't need money when you got muscles, 'cause you can just take a nigga shit.

Eddie nodded. "I see yo' point. Who dis?" he asked, looking Cherry up and down.

"This my baby girl, Cherry. Cherry, this Eddie. She gon' help me work out that situation with them ho-ass Savages. My baby get down, too," Dirty said, patting her on the ass.

Eddie grinned. "That's what I wanted to hear. C'mon. Let's get the fuck outta this airport. I got y'all a li'l crib already. I'ma take y'all there so y'all can drop y'all shit off and get situated. After that, y'all wit' me for the night. Show y'all how we ball out in the Mil!"

"Yeah, all that sound good. But where them pistols at I told you I needed? I don't like riding around without my shit. I feel naked."

"My nigga Keese got 'em. He gon' get wit' us after y'all get situated. I got y'all a house on Burleigh. Them niggas call it The Zoo. Bunch of wild niggas over there that be fuckin' shit up. Dirty, you should feel right at home."

***

Dirty and Cherry's living arrangement was the upper level of a fully-furnished duplex. The lower level housed two females that eyed Dirty like he was a superstar.

After checking their new spot and dropping their bags off, Eddie took them out on the town. They ended up at a strip club downtown called Angels. They partied, got drunk, and threw money on strippers. About an hour into their partying, Keese showed up.

"Dirty, this my nigga, Keese. Keese, this my cousin I was tellin' you about. My nigga get down for real," Eddie said, introducing the men.

Dirty looked Keese over from head to toe. He was tall, standing six-foot-four, skinny, brown-skinned, hair cut low, face clean-shaved except for a little mustache. He looked to be in his early twenties.

"What it do, my nigga?" Dirty nodded.

"Shit. You got it. My nigga Eddie told me how you was fuckin' shit up in Minnesota."

Dirty smiled. "When I see a pussy-nigga, that shit get my dick hard. You got them burners?"

"Yeah. They outside. Two Glock 17s and a AR-15. How that sound?"

"Shit, sound like you 'bout to be my nigga," Dirty said, handing him the bottle of Remey from the table. "Pull up a seat and drank with a nigga."

"Fa sho!"

"Y'all tell me more about these Savage niggas. Who they is and where they be?" Dirty asked.

"It was four of them niggas, but somebody faded one of them niggas a li'l while back. Ain't heard nothing about who did it, either. Them niggas been out here fuckin' shit up for so long that it coulda been anybody," Eddie explained

"Dro, Twenty, and Lunatic. Tae the one that got knocked off. Niggas used to be over on Garfield, but ever since them prices been on them niggas' heads, ain't nobody been seein' 'em. But make no mistake about it, them niggas get down. They got plenty bodies under they belt. And they plugged with this pimp nigga, The Ho Whisperer. It's Lunatic's uncle," Keese explained.

"The Ho Whisperer?" Cherry laughed.

"On what you didn't just make that nigga name up?"

Dirty chuckled.

"That's the nigga name, for real," Eddie spoke up. "Pimp nigga checkin' a bag, too. Nigga been in them old pimp DVDs back in the day. He valid. Shit, you can Google that nigga and some of his videos pop up."

A light shown in Dirty's eyes. "So, why ain't none of yo' shooters just lamped on The Ho Whisperer and clapped these niggas up? They can't be that hard to find if the nigga uncle got a spotlight on him that bright."

Eddie and Keese looked dumbfounded.

"That's why we here, baby," Cherry spoke up.

Eddie nodded. "She right. That's why y'all here."

Dirty took a few moments to think. "A'ight. This gotta be the easiest money I ever got. Shit simple. This how we gon' do it. Since he pimpin', we can catch a few of the nigga hos. We can make up a reason to party and get some of them hos to come through. If The Ho Whisperer show up, we can get on some gangsta shit and kidnap the nigga and make his nephew come out and off both they ass. Or, plan B is Cherry. Baby, you could make yo'self available during the party and make sure they notice you. Choose that nigga and let him take you home. Learn where them niggas be and how they move. Then, when the time is right, it's over."

Eddie nodded in agreement. "I like the second one better. That information on all them niggas is what we need."

"I like the second one, too," Keese spoke up. "Bag all them niggas instead of The Ho Whisperer and his nephew."

"What you think, baby?" Dirty asked Cherry.

"I think we should get a down payment. As an incentive. I'm finna put my ass in the line of fire, and I don't wanna do it for nothing."

"I like how you think, baby," Dirty smiled before turning to Eddie. "I need that down payment, and we gon' get on them niggas ASAP."

"I ain't the one payin' them tags. Monster li'l brother is."

"Well, call that nigga and tell him what I said. If he want them niggas out the way, show us how serious he is. I showed up, so y'all know I'm ready."

Eddie thought for a moment before nodding to Keese. "Okay. Call that nigga right now."

While Keese made the call, Dirty addressed unfinished business with his cousin. "So, how you was out here eatin' and gettin' fat, but you didn't reach back for me while I was on lock? That was some real fuck-nigga shit, cuz."

Regret flashed in Eddie's eyes. "Damn, my nigga. I know that was some fuck-shit. I don't even know what to say. The truth is, I was out here living fast. On some selfish shit. I thought about you, but I didn't do shit about it."

"That's a bullshit-ass excuse, my nigga. You thought about me, but didn't think to shoot a nigga a money order? I did seven years. I almost rather you lied than tell me some ho-ass shit like that."

"One thing I ain't gon' do is lie to you, my nigga. We blood. But I got a li'l package for you. Here you go." Eddie pulled a stack of bills from his pocket and sat in on the table. "That's ten. It's all you."

Dirty eyed his cousin as he picked up the money. "I'ma accept this from you. But just know this don't take away my disappointment. I'm out here now, so I don't need no handouts. I'ma run it up myself. I just want you to know that wasn't no real-nigga shit. And if we wasn't blood cousins, I woulda fucked you up already. But I'ma let that shit go."

"Coupe said he on his way over to us," Keese said after hanging up the phone. "He said he wanna meet y'all and holla in person."

Coupe showed up to Angels thirty minutes later. He

wasn't what Dirty was expecting. Coupe was a little nigga, five-foot-two-inches and light in the ass. Wore gold-rimmed buffs, had gold teeth, and an uncombed Philly fro. He was with a butch chick named Levi who looked like his twin.

"'Sup wit' chu niggas?" Coupe asked, greeting everyone at the table.

"Waiting on you," Eddie spoke up. "This my cousin, Dirty, and his girl, Cherry. They gon' take care of the Savages."

Coupe looked Dirty over and wasn't impressed. "It's just you? You don't got no team?"

"I don't need one. Too many niggas mean too many witnesses. Less is more, nigga. It's plenty of us."

"You know these niggas ain't no joke, right? They certified."

Dirty let out a snort. "Check this out, my nigga. I don't mean no disrespect, but all I been hearing about since I showed up is how beasty these Savage niggas is. Like y'all scared of these niggas or something. I ain't neva met a nigga that don't bleed. Niggas ain't bulletproof. I don't need a clique of niggas, and I don't draw off numbers. I told Eddie that we need a down payment, and me and my baby gon' take care of these niggas. Talk money, my nigga. I don't got time for nothin' else."

Coupe looked to Levi. She nodded. "I'm paying fifty a head. I'ma advance you twenty-five. Give you the other twenty-five when you put one of them niggas in a box. How that sound?"

Dirty extended a hand. "Sound like I'm finna get paid."

After kicking it at the club for a few more hours and getting faded, Dirty and his woman walked outside to get their money and guns. They stopped at Coupe's Audi truck first.

128

"Here you go, my nigga. Get at me when you make that move," Coupe said, handing him twenty-five Gs.

Dirty smiled, shaking his hand. "Fuck with me, you know I got it."

Next he walked over to Keese's Yukon truck. On the back seat was a black duffle bag. Keese opened it, showing the weapons. There were two Glocks with thirty-round clips, and the AR-15 had a drum attached. Seeing the assault rifle made Dirty smile.

"These bitches look good!" he grinned, throwing the money in the bag before zipping it closed.

"They clean, too. Brand new," Keese told him.

"My nigga!" Dirty smiled, giving him a hug before taking the bag.

Eddie was standing next to his black Range Rover. When Dirty approached, he tossed him the keys. "Take care of my baby."

Dirty looked at his cousin, and then the truck. "This me?"

"Yeah, nigga. I'm feeling guilty as fuck for not reaching back while you was on lock. Hopefully this take away some of that animosity."

Dirty hugged his cousin. "Hell yeah! Good lookin' out, nigga. I'ma take this shit home and get with you later. You need a ride?"

"Nah. I'ma jump in wit' Keese. I'ma find a way to get in contact with The Ho Whisperer and hit you later. Love."

Cherry drove away from the strip club, using the GPS to find her way to their new house. "Them niggas showed us love," she said, loving the smooth ride of the luxury truck.

"That's cause they some bitch-ass niggas, and they know I'm 'bout that action. I'm thinking about tearing all they asses off before we leave. Set this bitch on fire," Dirty grinned.

"I'm with it. That's how you really run up a check."

When the Rover pulled up to their new house, the first thing they noticed was the niggas sitting on the porch. There were four of them sitting on the steps. One of the females from downstairs was kicking it with them.

"Fuck is this shit?" Dirty cursed, wishing he didn't have the duffle bag filled with guns and money.

"Damn, baby. I think yo' cousin put us in a trap," Cherry commented as they climbed from the SUV.

"We ain't finna do this," he mugged as they walked toward the house. "These niggas finna have to move around."

When they walked to the porch, the niggas mugged him and Cherry, not even moving out of the way so they could get past.

"You niggas ain't gon' move?" Dirty asked, getting hostile.

They all began standing up. "Who is you, nigga?"

Dirty stuck a hand inside the bag slung over his shoulder, gripping a Glock. "I'm Dirty, nigga. And this my house."

One of the niggas further away spoke up. "We don't give no fuck. This The Zoo. Everythang in The Zoo ours. Even yo' house."

"And what you got in that bag, nigga?" another one spoke up, moving a hand toward the bulge in his waist. "Take yo' hand out before I get nervous."

Dirty looked around at the mugs on the niggas' faces and knew what time it was. A couple of them had bulges under their shirts. He wanted to demonstrate with the AR, but knew he wouldn't be able to get it out of the bag before the niggas pulled their pistols.

After giving Cherry a quick look, she spun toward the SUV. Dirty pulled a Glock from the bag and shot the closest nigga to him in the face. Before the body hit the ground, Dirty backpedaled toward the Range Rover, letting the Glock ride.

The downstairs neighbor screamed as the niggas ran from the porch. One of the niggas with the bulge pulled his heat, ducking behind a porch pillar and popping back. Dirty had more bullets, and when he pulled the other Glock, the nigga had to duck out of the way or get his shit knocked off.

By the time he made it to the truck, Cherry was already inside with the engine running.

"Bitch-ass niggas!" Dirty screamed, pulling out his phone and calling Eddie. "Where you at, nigga? I just had to get down on some pussy-ass niggas."

"Hold on. What the fuck you talkin' 'bout?"

"I'm talkin' 'bout that trap house you put us in. Them Zoo niggas was waiting on my porch. I just got into a shootout with them niggas. We need another house. And don't put us in the hood."

J-Blunt

Chapter 12

"I need you young hyenas to keep y'all eyes open. It's something about this nigga that don't feel right," The Ho Whisperer said, reclining in the plush seat of the limousine.

"Why you meeting with the nigga if you got a funny feeling?" Lunatic asked.

"Because he wanna talk money. That's my language. But I'm leery. Something just don't feel right."

"You know I got you, Whisper," Twenty spoke up. "I'll pop his ass in front of everybody at the party if he get on some ho-ass shit."

"It ain't gon' be like that. I don't expect shit to pop off. But I want y'all ready, just in case. A'ight? And Luna, this can be yo' playground. It should be a lot of misguided potentials up in here. Let's see if anything I told you stayed in that thick-ass head of yours."

Lunatic grabbed at the lapels on the tailored black suit and adjusted the Cartier glasses on his face. "I'ma tell you something, Unc. I think when it's all said and done, they gon' write books about how pimpish I was. Matter fact, before I'm done they gon' write the first book. Shit, I might start lookin' for a ghost writer after we leave this party. Tonight is the birth of Flex. That's my new name. What you think?"

"I think you smoked something other than weed on the way over," Twenty laughed.

"Stay who you are. Don't let this shit change you before you start. The most effective people are the ones that stay grounded in themselves. If you start thinking like some nigga named Flex, you might lose the nigga you spent all those years growing up to be," The Ho Whisperer said.

Lunatic nodded at the wise words. "I was just bullshitting. You know I'ma stay Lunatic. This Savage shit gon' always be a part of me."

"Now that's the nigga I know," Twenty nodded. "Bet' not let this pimp shit take away that Savage heart."

"It's in me, my nigga, not on me," Lunatic said confidently.

When they stepped inside Virgil's, the first thing they noticed was the sign stating WELCOME HOME CARTER!!! The night club held about fifty people. It had been rented out by Keese to throw a private party for his nigga who had come home from a five-year bid. When Whisper walked in with the women, all eyes flocked to the new arrivals. The women posed and postured while Whisper looked for the man who made the arrangements.

"The Ho Whisperer! What it do, baby?"

Whisper sized up the nigga that called his name. He was light-skinned, stood average height, and had an uncombed afro and a potbelly. "What's up, brotha?"

"You got it. I'm Eddie," the chubby nigga said, extending a hand and eyeing the women. "I see you brought out the bad ones."

"When you said you wanted my finest, I delivered." Whisper said before turning to his flock. "Ladies, I think they waiting on y'all. Show em why we came."

The women sauntered away and went right to work on the partygoers. Eddie watched the professionals walk away, his eyes so focused on their asses that he forgot about Whisper, Lunatic, and Twenty.

"You got somewhere we can talk?" Whisper asked, getting his attention. "You said you wanted to meet with me, right?"

"Oh, yeah. Fa sho. My bad. You got some nice-looking females," he recovered before leading Whisper to a table.

"Lunatic, you and Twenty look around while I talk

business," Whisper said as he had a seat at the table.

"You want something to drink?" Eddie offered, pointing to the bottle of Ciroc on the table.

"For sure," The pimp said, pouring himself a glass. "Where do I know you from?"

Eddie looked caught off guard. "We never met before. I don't think. At least I don't remember it."

Whisper ran a hand across his goatee. "You look familiar. I've seen you before. I just can't remember where. It'll come to me. So, what kinda business do you want to discuss?"

"Well, I hear you the man to talk to if I want exotic dimes. And based on what you brought to the party, I can see that I'm talking to the right nigga. I'm starting a magazine, and I need some bitches. Not just any bitches, but the best of the best. Bad bitches."

Whisper gave an unimpressed look, expecting more. "That's why you wanted to meet? Seriously?"

Eddie looked uncomfortable. "Yeah. I was hoping we could talk some numbers and do a li'l contract or somethin'."

Whisper nodded. "What's the name of the mag, and when do it come out?"

"It's called *Ready*. And I wanna drop in the next six months. I wanna target niggas in the joint. Them skin magazines be doin' numbers. *Straight Stuntin'* and *Thick* the hot ones, and niggas on lock need them hos. We gon' move them at fifteen dollars a pop."

"Okay. When you ready to do the shoot, we can work out something. We got time."

"I like the sound of that. Let's shake on it," Eddie grinned, extending a hand. "So, what is it gon' take to get you to stay for a li'l while and turn up wit' us? It ain't every day niggas get to kick it with a real-life pimp."

***

Across the room, Twenty and Lunatic stood at the bar, watching the partygoers and sipping drinks.

"I know you geeked about putting that case behind you," Twenty said.

"Man, you don't even know," Lunatic grinned, watching a thick, dark-skinned female dancing sexually to the music. "Case closed with self defense. Brandon a beast, bro. No bullshit. That nigga got the job done."

"What you think about Dro? You think he murked Tae."

Lunatic let out a breath. "I don't know. He said he didn't do it, and I wanna believe him. But that nigga different. Ever since Asia got killed, I don't feel like I know him."

"Same shit. It's like he don't fuck wit' us no more. Only reason I'm givin' him the benefit of the doubt is because he didn't know where Tae was staying."

"Yeah. The nigga was getting out the street before, so I don't put too much stock in him not wantin' to fuck with us tonight. But on some other shit, you see this chocolate bitch? She bad as fuck and been in my face since we walked in the door."

"I thought she was lookin' at me," Twenty said, eyeing the woman Lunatic was talking about. She wore a tight red dress, her big-ass titties spilling out the top.

"Well, let me go over there and see. Pour this pimp juice in her cup," Luna cracked before walking out on the dance floor. He went up to the woman and whispered in her ear. She smiled before walking with him to the bar.

"My name Lunatic. What's yours?"

"Shay. Can I get a drink?"

Lunatic nodded to the barkeeper. "She want a drink, man."

"A Sex On The Beach."

"You know drinks ain't free?" Luna fished.

"Neither is my time. Who is yo' friend?" she asked, looking toward Twenty.

"That's my nigga, Twenty. But why you worried about anotha nigga and I'm standing right here?"

"He was watching me watch you, and I'm 'bout my money."

Luna realized he was dealing with a pro. "You came here trynna catch a date, huh?"

She smiled. "I gotta get mines, baby."

He liked the boldness of her hustle. "Listen, Shay. I'm in the same line of business that you in. And I'm connected. Fuck wit' me and I can take you to the next level so you won't have to be at parties trynna catch a date at the bar. I came in wit' a flock that catch flights to different cities. Choose me and you can be on the next flight."

She looked Luna up and down. "Sorry, baby, but I ain't lookin' for no pimp. I make my own money."

"I ain't no pimp, shawty. I'm a manager. I got the connection, and you got the goods. In the real world, that's called coming together for a exchange of goods and service. Or business."

She smiled. "I ain't gon' lie, That was a good pitch. Tell you what, gimme yo' number and we can talk more about this later. Right now I need to catch a check, and it's a nigga over there that ain't stopped looking at me since I left the dance floor."

***

"I think I caught a great white, Unc," Lunatic smiled.

"I seen you over there by the bar. She look independent. Seen her talk to at least three niggas. Now she over there with

Twenty," Whisper said, nodding across the room.

Twenty sat in a chair next to Shay. It looked like they were laughing it up and having a good time.

"She trynna catch a bag. I like her drive. I told her I got some opportunities for her. She bit. I'ma need yo' help putting her on some fast cash moves."

"I think you should let that one go. Throw that fish back in the water. You don't gotta keep the first bite."

"It's somethin' 'bout that one, Unc. I want her."

"See, that's the problem. You wanna fuck her. That ain't the goal, Nephew. You gotta look at a bitch as an investment, not somebody you wanna fuck. If you let yo' dick do the talkin', you gon' be broke. You let her seduce you, and that's backwards. Pimps don't get seduced. We seducers. Throw that one back, Nephew. Trust me on this one."

Lunatic wasn't convinced. Whisper was right that he did want to fuck Shay. She was fine, had some big titties, and a phat ass. But that wasn't why he wanted to keep her. What had him most interested was her drive. She was a go-getter. And if he could knock her as his first hoe, the sky was the limit.

***

"How that shit go?" Dirty asked when Cherry hopped in the passenger seat of the Rover.

"I got both them niggas, baby. Lunatic wanna be my pimp, and Twenty wanna fuck. He thirsty, so we could probably get him tonight."

Dirty smiled, visualizing his pockets being a hundred thousand dollars richer. "You makin' this way too easy. I seen you over there putting in work, but I didn't know you was this good. Shit ain't fair."

"I know. But I like having the advantage. So, how you wanna play it, baby?"

"I think we gon' play it like you said. Call Twenty. Get a room. Leave the door unlocked. Me and Keese gon' come through."

***

Twenty took one last look around before knocking on the motel door. When it opened, Cherry stood in the doorway wearing a white negligée.

"Hey, baby," she smiled, opening her arms for a hug.

Twenty palmed her phatty during the embrace before stepping into the room. "See you looking and smelling good as a mu'fucka."

"Presentation is a part of the Shay experience," she grinned before closing the door.

"Go 'head and lock that," Twenty told her.

"Okay. But we good. You don't got nothing to worry about but hittin' this pussy and letting me suck that dick," she said, pausing a split second before twisting the lock, but not actually locking the door.

"I know. But I'm a hot boy," Twenty said, glancing at the door as he sat on the bed. "How we doin' this?"

She stood before him with hands on her hips. "You tell me. How you want it? How long you wanna stay?"

Twenty lay back on the bed. "Shit, I got all night. Let me see yo' best moves."

Cherry got down on her knees and started crawling on the carpet. While on her knees, she did some sexy body rolls before spinning around and making her ass bounce. When she knew he was good and turned on, she lay on her back, spreading her legs wide. After sliding the negligée aside, she exposed her fat, bald pussy and began fingering herself.

Twenty was mesmerized by the sexy show, dick harder than steel.

"You want some of this?" she asked, sticking a finger in her mouth and tasting her own juices.

Twenty grabbing his dick through the pants. "Hell yeah!"

"Let me see what you working with."

Twenty pulled the .357 automatic with an extended clip from his pants and sat it next to him on the bed before stripping out of his clothes. Cherry got on her knees and crawled over to him.

"You don't need that no more," she said, eyeing the hand cannon.

Twenty refused to part with his bitch. "Yes, I do. Don't worry about my pistol. Worry about that," he said, nodding toward his dick.

Cherry moved closer, kneeling between his legs and sliding his dick between her lips.

"Aw, shit!" Twenty groaned, leaning his head back and closing his eyes.

Cherry bobbed her head up and down rapidly, all the while trying to think of a way to separate him from the gun. It was next to his thigh, but she didn't want to touch it for fear of making him suspicious.

"Damn, baby. Suck that mu'fucka," Twenty groaned, grabbing the back of her head and pushing it down so she could deep throat.

Cherry didn't disappoint. She climbed onto the bed and deep throated him while playing with his balls. Figuring he was distracted, she pushed the gun off the bed. It landed on the carpeted floor with a thud.

Twenty's eyes shot open. When he seen his pistol on the floor, he reached down for it.

At that moment the motel door opened. Keese was the first one in the room, wearing a mask and gloves, pistol at the ready. But Cherry being in the way made him pause, and that was his mistake.

Twenty rolled off the bed, snatching up the .357 and letting it ride.

Bocca, bocca, bocca, bocca!

Keese caught all four of the slugs in his chest and torso. Before his body could hit the ground, Dirty dashed into the room. He also wore a mask and gloves, but unlike Keese, he wasn't worried about shooting Cherry.

Pop, pop, pop, pop, pop!

Twenty felt the bullets rip through his leg and stomach as he returned fire. The .357 sounded like thunder as it roared in the small hotel room, tearing chucks out of the walls.

Dirty knew he couldn't compete with the fire power. He also couldn't get a good shot at Twenty, so he did the only thing he could do and got the fuck out of the room.

"Ah!" Cherry screamed, grabbing her clothes and making a run for the door.

"Nah, bitch!" Twenty said, lifting the tramp and squeezing the trigger twice. The bullets hit her in the back, slamming her into the wall where she fell to the floor.

Twenty struggled to get to his feet, using the bed to help him stand. Cherry tried to crawl toward the door. Twenty lifted the .357 one more time, taking aim at her head.

Bocca!

The slug slapped into the back of her head, opening a wide crater and painting the floor with her brains.

J-Blunt

Chapter 13

"How you doin' today, Unc?" Dro asked as Crush climbed in the Charger.

"I don't know, Nephew. One of them days," Crush sighed as he sat heavily in the passenger seat.

"What's going on, man? Talk to me."

Crush was silent for a moment, thinking. "I'm lonely, man. I want my family back. While I was in jail, I pictured this nice reunion between me, Candice, and Kathy. Like in the movies, you know? I got clean and figured everything would go back to how it was. Didn't figure on Candice moving on."

Dro gave a chuckle at the expense of his love-sick uncle. "Damn, Unc. I feel yo' pain, man. Ain't nothing you can do but move on yo'self. They say the only way to get over somebody is to get somebody else."

"That ain't always true, Nephew. I haven't been with Candice in five years, and I'm still in love with her. I've been with a lotta women during that time, but none of them could ever take her place or make me forget her. She is the one for me. The only one. I'm tired of sleeping alone in that apartment. I want my family back."

"I think you should let her have what she got with Billy. She happy. Love her from a distance and just be there for her when she needs you. Ain't nothing you can do about it now, man."

"I been thinking about killing him."

Dro took his eyes off the road to look at his uncle. "You not serious, is you?"

Crush blew out a breath. "I'm not gon' do it. That would be a selfish-ass sucka move. And it would hurt Candice. I've brought enough pain to her life. I'm just telling you I thought about it."

"Damn, Unc. That love bug is the truth, huh?"

Crush let out a little laugh. "Yeah, man. It ain't no joke. What you got going on today? Anybody heard from Twenty?"

"Nah. Nigga still MIA. This ain't like him, either. I hope nothing ain't happened to my nigga."

"He okay. He might just be taking a vacation from all the madness."

"I hope so."

"So, what's going on with you and America? Have you talked to her since the big fight?"

"Nah. Don't plan on it, either. It's crazy that I used to love that girl, and now I can't stand her. She came over there wiggin' out. She lucky I didn't kill her and that pussy-ass nigga of hers."

"Well, she did stumble on you fucking her best friend. Hard to take that kind of news lightly."

"I don't give a fuck. She shoulda handled it better and not put her hands on me."

"I hear you, Nephew. But you might wanna talk to her. Y'all both experienced a great loss and might need to help each other get past it. Ain't Asia's birthday coming up soon?"

Dro nodded. "Yeah. In ten days. I don't know how I'ma be on that day. She would've turned nine. But fuck America. I'm good. She can do her, and I'ma do me."

Dro's phone vibrating made him pause. He didn't recognize the number showing on the screen. "Hello?"

"Dro, I'm fucked, my nigga," Twenty said. "I need a lawyer."

"Fuck you at, nigga? We been lookin' for you for three days."

"I'm downtown. They got me in a jam, brah. Niggas tried to get me out the way and shot me up. Holla at Brandon and send him down here."

"Okay. I'ma do that when I get off the phone. What the fuck happened? Who is the niggas?"

"I can't talk on this phone. I still ain't got booked yet. Tell Luna that bitch from the party set me up. He know what I'm talkin' about. They finna charge me wit' a couple bodies. Send Brandon. I'ma get at you once I get in the booking room. Put some money on yo' phone."

"I got you, my nigga. I'ma call Brandon ASAP and get at Luna. Love, my nigga. Stay dangerous."

"Love. Savage."

"What's goin' on, Nephew?" Crush asked after he hung up the phone.

Dro looked like the world around him was on fire. "That was Twenty. He locked up. Some niggas shot him up. They charging him with a couple bodies. Said a bitch set him up."

Crush eyes got wide like he took a blast from a crack pipe stuffed with an eight ball. "What? What the fuck is going on?"

"I don't know. He couldn't say that much because he was on they phone. I gotta call this lawyer," Dro mumbled, searching his phone for Brandon's number. "Brandon, this Ruben. My boy in a jam, and he need a lawyer."

"Okay. Where is he?"

"Down at the county. Said he being charged for murder, and he got shot. He need you, like, yesterday."

"Okay. Gimme his name."

"Kevin Cooper."

"Okay. I'll get down there within the hour."

After hanging up with the lawyer, Dro called Lunatic.

"What it do, Dro?"

"Brah, Twenty just called me. He locked up. I just called Brandon to go represent him."

Lunatic couldn't believe what he heard. "What? On what?

What he locked up for?"

"Said he caught some bodies. Where you at?"

"I'm at the condo. You said bodies? More than one?"

"That's what he said. I'm on my way."

When Dro and Crush walked in the condo, Lunatic sat on the couch wearing a look of disbelief. "What all that nigga say?"

"He said that bitch from the party set him up. Fuck he talkin' 'bout?"

"He talkin' 'bout Shay?" Lunatic asked.

"I don't know. He said you knew."

"That's who he talkin' 'bout," Whisper spoke up from his seat across the room. "I told you that bitch wasn't no good. I knew she was a snake."

Dro looked to the pimp, wanting to be in the loop. "What the fuck y'all talkin' 'bout?"

"The party you didn't wanna come to with us. We met a badass bitch that was trynna catch a check. I was trynna get the bitch on some pimp shit. She was moving back and forth, working the room. Damn, I can't believe that bitch set up my nigga," Lunatic said, wearing the astonishment on his face.

Dro pulled out his phone and began checking local news sites, reading the shootings over the last couple of days. He ran across one that caught his eye. "I think I found it. It was a triple shooting at the Days Inn. A man and a woman died. Another man was shot and is in police custody. Said they wasn't releasing no names."

Silence filled the living room as everyone got lost in thought.

"You think this about them numbers on y'all heads, or a bitch looking for a paycheck?" Crush asked.

Dro shook his head. "I don't know, Unc."

"I'ma work on getting that video footage from the club.

This might be bigger than we think," Whisper spoke up.

***

It felt like déjà vu. Dro sat next to Crush and Lunatic in a pew at the back of the courtroom. He had been in these exact same seats with Tae and Twenty coming to Lunatic's court hearing. This time he was waiting for Twenty's hearing to begin.

As he sat, Dro couldn't help but think of his own impending court date. It was a motion hearing two weeks from today. The thought of spending time in a cell made his skin crawl. He hated jail and never wanted to go back. He could only imagine how his nigga felt. Like Dro, Twenty was already a felon. He wasn't supposed to be in possession of a gun. And the fact two people died only made the situation worse. It wasn't looking good for the home team. If it was possible for Twenty to get bail, they planned on anteing up and getting him out. But considering the seriousness of the situation, Dro didn't get his hopes up.

At 9:15 the side door opened and Twenty was wheeled into the courtroom, strapped to a wheelchair. He wore an orange jumpsuit, his dreads in a ponytail. There were no obvious signs he was hurt, but underneath the jumpsuit there were bandages on his leg and stomach.

The assistant district attorney read the criminal complaint. "Your honor, this is cut and dry. Mr. Cooper shot and killed two people inside the Days Inn Motel. He shot Spencer Bridges in the chest four times, and he also shot Cherry King three times, twice in the back and once in the back of the head. He was also wounded in the gun battle. He was apprehended trying to flee the scene. The state recommends he be held with no bail until trial."

"Your honor, Mr. Thurman is misrepresenting the facts," Brandon Williams shouted. "My client was ambushed and fired in self defense. The woman, Cherry King, set him up to be robbed. The deceased, who was wearing a mask and gloves, was her partner. Witnesses say another man wearing a mask and carrying a gun also ran from the room. We request a bail in the interest of fairness. My client shot in self defense. He was almost killed, for goodness sakes."

The court commissioner was silent for a moment as he read the complaint and looked Twenty over. "This is a difficult case because the defendant was clearly the victim of a crime. But he shot two people multiple times, one of them an unarmed female. He is also a felon in possession of a firearm. I will set the initial bail at $250,000 cash and have the case bound over for trial."

***

"I think he gon' beat the charges. They did the same shit to me when I got popped," Lunatic said from the back seat of the Charger. "You know these DAs gotta overcharge niggas to try to make something stick. Luckily for me I wasn't a felon. They had to drop my body count."

"That's what I think gon' stick," Dro said as he pulled up to a red light. "I think that's how they gon' get me, too."

"I don't know if he gon' beat two homicides. If he shot one person, maybe. But when the judge mentioned the female was unarmed, that was a red flag for me," Crush said.

Dro and Lunatic gave him sour looks.

"C'mon, Unc. We trynna speak positive about my nigga."

"I know, man. Can't be talkin' like that and puttin' some bad juju in the air. Don't do that."

"Man, y'all real sensitive," Crush shrugged. "I was just

adding my two cents."

"Save that shit and put it towards yo rent." Lunatic said. "Gotta lace Crush on real nigga etiquette, Dro."

Dro didn't respond to the comment. He was too busy watching the rearview mirror. "Any of y'all got something y'all ain't supposed to have?"

"Nah, why?" Crush asked, turning to look out the back window.

"Don't turn around!" Dro warned.

Too little, too late.

"Oh, shit! The Po-Po!" Crush panicked.

"I don't got shit," Lunatic said calmly. You got yo' license, right?"

Dro continued to watch the rearview mirror. "Yeah. We good. I'm just making sure you niggas didn't have shit. It look like they running the plates."

"All yo' paperwork in order?" Crush asked.

"Yeah. It's registered –"

Whoop, whoop! The siren sounded, making Dro swallow his words.

He pulled to the side of the road and parked. The police cruiser pulled right up to the bumper, and both officers got out, hiding behind their doors, pointing their weapons.

"Driver! Cut the engine and stick your hands out the window!" the officer called over the bullhorn.

"Dro, what the fuck you do, nigga?" Lunatic asked, a tenor of fear in his voice.

"I didn't do shit nigga. They on some bullshit," Dro said, trying to decide what his next move would be. Something was wrong, and he was considering a high-speed chase.

"Driver, do what the fuck I said or I'm going to blow your fucking head off!"

"You heard him, Nephew. Getcho hands up," Crush said,

raising his hands high.

Dro pulled out his phone. "Wait. I gotta call Brandon. I don't like this shit," he said before dialing his lawyer. He didn't answer, so he left a message. "Brandon, I'm gettin' pulled over on Highland Street. Police got the guns out. Come over as soon as you get this message."

Four more police cars came on the scene, boxing the Charger in. All the police jumped out, pointing guns at the car.

"*Driver, show me your fucking hands!*"

"Okay! Okay!" Dro complied, sticking his hands out the window.

"*Both passengers do the same! Stick your hands out the windows!*"

Lunatic and Crush followed the orders.

"*Driver, open the door slowly and lay face down on the ground! Keep your hands where we can see them!*"

Dro moved slowly from the car, keeping his hands in plain view. While he lay face down on the ground, he did something he hadn't done in long time. Prayed. He prayed to God the police wouldn't get trigger happy and gun him down in the street.

"*Passenger, open the door slowly and lay face down on the ground! Keep your hands where we can see them!*"

When Crush got on the ground, they gave Lunatic the same order. After all the men were face down in the street, they were cuffed and searched.

"What's going on, man? Why y'all pull me over?" Dro asked as he was shoved in the back of a police car.

"For riding around in a stolen car. Where'd you get it?"

Dro frowned. "What? Man, that's my car. Y'all got the wrong person. That car ain't stolen."

"According to a police report filed two days ago, that car

is stolen," the cop said. "You got any drugs or guns in the vehicle?"

"Nah. It's clean. I just came back from court. Y'all made a mistake. That's my car."

The cop studied Dro for a moment before hitting the button on his radio. "Hey, Grant, you wanna search the car? Get a dog if you can. I'm gonna talk to the suspect driver."

"I got it," the radio chattered.

"Where did you get the car?" he asked.

"I bought it off the car lot. That's my car," Dro said adamantly.

"And when did you buy this car?"

"Almost two years ago. This is a mistake."

After one more long look, the cop opened the passenger door and sat in the seat. He tapped a key on the laptop. "I'm gonna show you that car was reported stolen, and you're gonna tell me the truth."

After a couple taps on the keyboard, he showed Dro the screen. The car was reported stolen. That's when it hit him. America did this shit as payback for him fucking Shamika and beating up Block.

"Man, this gotta be a mistake. The car is in my daughter's mother's name. America Jones. Call her. This some kind of mix-up."

"That's not my job, brother. I track down the stolen rides and leave the rest to the lawyers and district attorneys. Right now I gotta take you down for operating a stolen vehicle. Whatever domestic problems you and your girl are having, you're going to have to work them out when you get out of jail."

J-Blunt

Chapter 14

"What the fuck, Brandon? You gotta get me outta here," Dro said, frustration spreading across his face as he paced the holding cell.

"I'm working on it. I might need a couple days for this one. You were out on bail, and they're most likely gonna hit you with bail jumping. It's gonna take a couple days to get you another bail."

"Bitch-ass shit!" he exploded, kicking the wall.

"I'm gonna talk to your kid's mother, too. See why she is doing this, and if I can get her to change her mind."

"She did it 'cause I fucked her friend and beat her boyfriend ass. Punk-ass bitch. Tell her if she don't drop that bullshit, I'ma bang her bitch-ass."

"C'mon, Ruben," Brandon laughed. "You know I'm not gonna do that. I'll use some diplomacy. Don't worry. I'll get you outta here."

Dro gave him a long stare. "A'ight, man. I'ma call you later. This some bullshit."

"I know, brotha. Take it easy, and don't get into trouble while you're in here. Man, you guys are keeping me busy. Glad y'all pay good."

***

After being booked in, Dro had to change into an orange jumpsuit provided by the county jail and trade his Nikes for a pair of shower sandals. When he was dressed in the inmate attire, two deputy sheriffs led him and five other niggas to a freight elevator. The ride was silent. The freedom-stripped men wore similar looks. Confusion. Despair. Devastation.

"Patrick, Wesley, and Green, you're going to 6A. Brown

and Card, you're going to 6B," the sheriff called when the elevator stopped.

Dro took the short walk down the hall, stopping at a big door. It was made of steel and plates of unbreakable glass in the top and bottoms of its frame. He could see into the unit from the hallway. All was quiet as the inmates were locked in their cells.

A loud clank sounded as the door unlocked. After walking in the unit, they stopped at the sheriff's desk. Dro looked around while the turnkey explained the rules and cell assignments. The pod was a large open space filled with a sea of chairs and tables. This was called the Dayroom. There were also two carpeted areas with chairs and TVs mounted on the walls. Two levels of cells surrounded the Dayroom. Thirty on the top and thirty on the bottom.

"Alright, guys. Wesley, you're in 28. Patrick, you're in 35. Brown, you're in 10. Dayroom opens after the noon count. I don't want no screaming out the cells, or you won't be coming out to my Dayroom. It's all about respect. Respect me and I'ma respect you. Disrespect me and we got a place for you. Go lock in."

Dro's room was upstairs. He took his time getting there, locking eyes with all the niggas that stared out their cells, hoping to see a familiar face. When he got to his cell, there was a linen roll sitting on a thin-ass mattress. Inside were blankets, sheets, and towels. A metal toilet and sink smelled of sterile cleaning supplies.

After closing the door, he made up the bed and lay down. It had been awhile since he was alone with his thoughts. There were no distractions in the cell. No phones, video games, or movies. Just him and his thoughts. Which went right to America. He wanted to kill her. Of all the punk-ass shit she could've done, taking a nigga's freedom was at the top of the list of shit not to do. That got people killed.

After hours of thinking on all the ways to kill his baby mama, his thoughts turned to Forever. He wanted to talk to her so bad right now, tell her he loved her and was sorry for the bullshit he was putting her through. His quest for vengeance had cost their relationship, and as much as he wanted to drop everything and go to her, he couldn't. His desire to kill J-Mac was too strong. He dreamed of killing the murderer of his daughter as much as dope boys dreamed of owning foreigns.

The State Fair shooting began playing in his head and he remembered the smile in J-Mac's eyes right before they started shooting.

"Dayroom!" the sheriff called.

When the door unlocked, Dro left the room, heading for the phone bank. A sea of niggas emerged from their rooms, going for the TV area, tables to play games, or phone banks. He looked around constantly as he descended the stairs, watching the faces of everyone, searching for potential enemies.

Then he spotted a face that made him smile. Twenty limped from a cell on crutches, heading for the phone bank.

"Twenty!"

His dreads flung wildly as he spun around to see who called his name. Surprise shown in his eyes when he seen Dro. "What the fuck you doin' in here, nigga?"

Dro walked over to hug his nigga. Besides the crutches, he looked well.

"America bitch-ass," he fumed. "Bitch reported my Charger stolen."

Twenty's eyes grew wide as full moons. "On what? Fuck she do that shit for?"

Dro shook his head. "She found out I was fuckin'

Shamika. They fought, and I whooped her nigga ass. Now they holding me on a bitch-ass bail jumping. Brandon said he gon' get me out in a couple days. But fuck what I'm doin'. What up wit' you? How the fuck you get popped?"

"Sit down with me so I can get off this leg," he said, walking over to an empty table. "The bitch was at a party. Bad-ass chocolate bitch that call herself Shay. Nigga named Eddie was throwing a party for some nigga gettin' out the joint. Whisper wanted me and Luna there 'cause he didn't trust the nigga or some shit. I see the bitch lookin' like she wanted to fuck. Me and Luna get at the bitch. She hit me up later and tell me to slide through the telly. When I walked in, I noticed the bitch didn't lock the door. That shit ain't seem right, especially for a ho bitch 'bout to turn a trick. I tell her to lock it, and she hesitated. I knew right then the bitch was on some bullshit, and I shoulda got up outta there. But I thought she locked the door, so I was like, 'Fuck it. I'ma keep my banger close and hit that shit and leave.' The bitch start suckin' my dick and knock my pistol on the floor. At the time I thought it was an accident, but looking back, I see the bitch wanted me naked. When I reached down to pick it up, the door opened. Turns out the bitch didn't lock the door all the way, or them niggas had keys 'cause they run in while I'm gettin my dick sucked. The first nigga paused 'cause I think the bitch was in the way. I fucked that nigga over, then another nigga run in and catch me in the stomach and leg. I blew at his bitch-ass, and he got up outta there. Bitch tried to run, and I blew her ass down at the door. I threw on my clothes and tried to get up outta there, but I was bleeding too much and movin' too slow. Feds was on a nigga. I thought about gettin' down on they ass, too, but I didn't have enough bullets."

"Damn, my nigga." Dro mumbled, looking blown away

by the story. "I'm glad you knocked that bitch shit out. Punk-ass bitch. Whisper was working on getting the video from the party. He think she might've been working with somebody at the party."

Twenty thought for a moment. "I thought about that, too. I was trynna think if somebody sic the bitch on us, because she was watchin' us as soon as we walked in that club. If all that shit was a set-up, that means niggas goin' through a lot to try to get us out he way."

"Niggas might be connected to Monster," Dro mumbled.

"Probably," Twenty nodded. "That means you niggas gotta watch y'all asses."

"I am. Did anybody interrogate you about Monster?"

"Nah, but I been thinking 'bout that shit. I didn't tell these mu'fuckas I had a alias."

"Good. Hopefully they don't figure that shit out. I'm a li'l annoyed about this weak-ass shit America pulled. If Jackson an' 'em find out I'm in here, they gon' be on my ass. I wanna kill that bitch dope-fiend ass."

"Dope fiend?" Twenty frowned.

"Yeah. Nigga Block got America snorting that defense."

"On what?" Twenty asked, shocked.

"That's what Shamika said. They ended up falling out right before I started fuckin' her."

Twenty shook his head. "Damn, my nigga. That's fucked up. But it might be good for you. Tell Brandon to give that bitch a few dollars to say she made that shit up. Get them charges dropped."

***

"Hi, Daddy!" Forever beamed, FaceTiming with her father.

"Hey, baby girl. What are you up to?"

"Nothing. Just came back from grocery shopping. I'm a little tired, so I was thinking about taking a nap."

"Okay. I won't hold you up long. I was thinking about you and thought I'd call. Wanted to know if you gave some more thought to moving back to North Dakota?"

"I've been thinkin' about it a lot, actually. I want to, but I can't make up my mind."

"It's Ruben, huh?"

"Yeah," she admitted, her bright and shining demeanor changing to storm clouds. "I don't want to give up on him, but I don't know how to get him back. He's changed since his daughter was killed."

"Yeah. I imagine losing a child could change a person."

"But it's made him worse. Before she died, he changed his life. Started going to church and gave his life to God. Now he's mad at God and all he thinks about is revenge on the man who did it. I love him, but I don't want him around me if he's going to kill someone."

"Do you really think he's capable of killing?"

She paused, remembering the conversations they had. "Yes."

"Well, I don't want you around anyone like that. Now, I really think you should come out here with me. I don't want you to get shot again. So, did he know the man who shot everybody?"

Forever didn't want to lie to her father, but she knew he wouldn't understand if she told the truth. And the truth would probably change her father's opinion of Ruben. She didn't want that. "No. But he knows people, and they are trying to help find him."

"I don't like the sound of this. I would feel a lot safer if you were here with me. Plus, you can't just think about yourself anymore. You're about to have –"

"Wait, Dad. Let me check my other line. Somebody is trying to call me. Hold on." After pausing her father, she answered the other line. "Hello?"

An automated voice told her she had a call from the Milwaukee County Jail. Then she heard Ruben's voice. Her heart raced, terrible thoughts popping into her mind as she accepted the call.

"Hey, Forever," Dro breathed.

"Why are you in jail? Are you okay?"

"Yeah. I'm good. Me and America got into it, and she reported my car stolen. They holding me. My lawyer is trying to get me bail, but said it might be a couple days."

"Why would she… wait. Can you hold on? My dad is on the other line. Let me tell him to call me back."

"A'ight."

After getting her father back on the phone she explained. "Dad, Ruben is on the other line and he's in jail. Can I call you back?"

"Yeah, baby. Is he okay?"

"Yeah. I think he is having problems with his daughter's mother."

"Okay. Call me when you finish talking to him. Tell him I said to keep his head up."

"I will. Bye, Daddy." After ending the call, she reconnected to Ruben. "Hello? Ruben?"

"Yeah. I'm still here."

"My dad says hi and to keep your head up."

"The next time you talk to him, tell him I said 'what's up?' How is he?"

"He's good. Wants me to move back to North Dakota."

The news surprised Dro. "For real?"

"Yeah. I've been thinking about it. I want to, but at the

same time I don't want to go."

"How long you been thinking about leaving?"

"I don't know. A few weeks."

"And you just now telling me?"

"Well, it's not like we talk all the time. You're out there doing God knows what. We go days and weeks without talking. You're the one who changed."

He let out a breath. "It's hard for me right now, Forever. You don't know what it feels like to lose a child. That shit changed me."

"I know. But that doesn't mean you push me away. We were supposed to be a team. Asia wasn't mine, and I can't imagine what it felt like to lose her, but we could've figured it out. And don't forget I got shot, too. I could've died. You didn't have to shut me out. We could've talked about me going back to North Dakota. You could've come with me, even. My dad wants me close to him, and I want to be with him, too. He thinks it's safer."

He was quiet for a moment. "You know, I never even thought about how you felt. I've been so caught up in my shit that I didn't even think about how you been feeling. I feel real shitty for that. I've been doing a lot of thinking since I been in here. Shit, I actually prayed. Surprised myself when I realized what I was doing."

"It means your heart is starting to soften. God is working. Genesis 50, verse 20 talks about what the devil meant for harm, God can turn it around and use it for good. America probably thought she was hurting you by doing what she did, but God is using this time to minister to your spirit. God hasn't given up on you."

"You wanna hear something crazy? A couple weeks ago this sidewalk preacher walked up to me and started talking about God is calling me. Then he said 'the life God put in me is larger than the life I'm living.' Something I heard Pastor McClain say. When he said it, it stopped me in my tracks."

"That's because God is still talking to you, baby. The calling is still on your life, Ruben. Remember when you told me it felt like God was watching you? Well, this is proof He is still watching."

"Then why he let my baby get killed? I can't get past that. I need a answer."

"Nobody can answer that but God."

Dro went silent for a moment. "I wanna see you when I get out."

The comment surprised Forever. "Um, I don't think that would be a good idea."

It was Dro's turn to be surprised. "Why not?"

"Because you still have your heart set on hurting the man who killed Asia."

"But what that gotta do with us?"

"Everything. You know what I believe in. God will avenge you. Let him fight your battle. I don't want you to bring any more drama in my life. That's how I got shot. I love you, but I don't want you putting my life in danger. Why can't you just walk away? Why can't you move to North Dakota with me and start over?"

"Because I can't. Hey, I gotta go. I'ma call you at the next day room."

J-Blunt

Chapter 15

It took Brandon four days and five hundred dollars to get Dro released from jail. After meeting with America and giving her the money, she signed the car title over and agreed to call the district attorney to drop the bogus charges. When the district attorney got the phone call and received the newly-signed car title as evidence, he released Dro immediately and threw out the charges.

For Dro, the date of his release came with a burden. Normally being freed from jail would be celebrated, but not on his daughter's birthday. He walked out of the jail with slumped shoulders and a sad disposition.

"Good morning, son. How are you feeling?" Marcia asked as he sat heavily on the passenger seat of her Blazer.

"Every time I got released from jail, I felt like celebrating. But today it just feels like I don't got nothing to celebrate. I miss my baby, and…." The tears choked away his words.

Marcia reached over to wrap her arms around her hurting son and kiss him atop the head. "I know, baby. We all miss her. But we gon' get through this as a family. We got you, baby."

From the county jail, Marcia drove to Asia's gravesite where family and friends gathered to visit the slain child on her birthday and pray. Missing from the event was America, and Dro was glad because he didn't know how he would react if he seen her face. But some of her family members did attend to show love.

After a sob fest at the graveyard, the blended family retreated to the church where her funeral was held and continued celebrating the life of Asia. By the time it was over, Dro was emotionally exhausted. After saying final goodbyes to family and friends, he ditched Crush and hopped in the

Charger.

During the drive, he called Forever.

"Hey."

"Why didn't you come to Asia's party? I needed you there. Why didn't you come?"

"C'mon, Ruben. We talked about this already. I told you I wasn't coming. That was for you and your family. I didn't want to rub anybody the wrong way. America might not've wanted me there. I didn't –"

"America didn't even come."

Forever couldn't hide her shock. "Wow. Are you serious?"

"Yeah. Her dope fiend-ass probably getting high with the money my lawyer gave her."

"Man, that is so wrong. Is she really on drugs?"

"Yeah. That's what I heard."

"That is messed up. How are you holding up? I know today has to be hard for you."

"I feel drained."

"I can hear it in your voice. Are you going home?"

"Nah. I'm pulling up to yo' house right now. I need to see you."

The was a slight pause by Forever. "What? You're where?"

"I'm parking in front of your building right now. Open the door."

"No, Ruben! I told you I didn't want to see you. Leave."

"I'm not leaving 'til I see you. Open the door," he said before hanging up the phone. After parking, he walked in the building, up to her apartment door and began knocking.

"I'm not opening the door, Ruben. Leave!" Forever called.

He began knocking louder. "I'm not leaving 'til I see you. Open the door."

"Ruben, stop! You're going to make my neighbors mad."

He continued knocking. "Well, open the door then."

"What's going on out here?"

Dro spun to face an older white lady that lived across the hall. "It's okay. I'm a friend."

"It doesn't look like she wants to be bothered. Why don't you leave?"

"Because I need to see her," he said before turning and knocking on the door again. "Forever, yo' neighbors coming out. Open the door."

"No, Ruben. Stop. You're embarrassing me. Leave," she whined.

"Didn't you hear what she said?" the old lady said. "She doesn't want to see you. You need to leave or I'm calling the police."

"Open the door, Forever. Yo' neighbor about to call the police. I know you ain't about to let me go back to jail."

"Rueben, why can't you just leave?" she cried.

"Not until you talk to me. Open the door."

"What's going on out here?" an Asian woman asked, appearing from an apartment two doors away.

"Romeo doesn't want to leave Juliet alone, and I'm about to call the police," the old lady said.

Excitement flashed in the Asian woman's eyes. "Ooh! Let me get my phone so I can record this."

"Forever, this is Gloria. Do you want me to call the police?" the white woman called.

"Grr!" Forever grunted. "No, Gloria. He's my boyfriend."

"Well, he can't stand in the hallway knocking all day and night, sweetie. You're going to have to talk to him or make him leave."

The Asian woman stepped into the hallway with her phone recording. "What did I miss?"

"Ruben, please leave. Don't do this," Forever called.

"I'm not leaving. Not until you talk to me. Open the door."

Forever paused. Dro began knocking on the door again.

"Okay! Okay! Give me a second to get dressed."

Dro and the old lady had a stare down while the Asian woman recorded it all.

"I'm sure there was an easier way to get her to open the door," Gloria said disdainfully.

"Maybe. But this worked. You can go back in your apartment now. Find you some business and get outta ours. And you can stop filming."

When the door finally opened, Forever began apologizing to her neighbors. "I'm sorry about this. I didn't know he was going to go this far."

"Are you sure you don't want me to call the police?" Gloria asked, looking Dro over from head to toe. "He looks like he might be trouble."

"No, I got it," she said before mugging Dro. "Get in here."

"You could've avoided all of that."

After locking the door, she spun to face him. "I told you I didn't want to see you. Why are you here?"

Dro stared at her for a moment, getting hypnotized by her beauty. It looked like God took his time crafting her DNA, making her the epitome of what the word 'beautiful' was supposed to represent. Hair flowing free with natural curls, slanted eyes blazing anger, and dimples that made a nigga's knees go weak every time she smiled. Today her skin seemed to be glowing, and even though she was covered up in a black jogging suit, she seemed to have gotten a little thicker.

"Because I missed you. And I wanted to see you. I need to talk to you."

"But what about what I wanted? I told you not to come over. Now my neighbors are going to be talking about me."

"You look really good," he said, catching her off guard with the compliment. And then he continued. "And I'm sorry you got shot because of me. And I'm sorry I pushed you away. I was just so mad. But after going to jail and getting together with the family today, I realized how important you are to me. The whole time everybody tried to comfort me, I wanted to push them away because the only person I wanted to comfort me was you. But you wasn't there 'cause I pushed you away. And I don't want to push you away no more. Asia dying changed me. I'm not saying that I expect everything to go back to the way it was, but I know I'm at my best when I'm with you. And who I am when I'm with you is who I wanna be."

His words had the healing effect of soothing balm on the skin of a burn victim. They melted away all of the walls she'd built up, poking her directly in the heart. She stood with her back against the door, tears spilling from her eyes, wanting to reach out and take ahold of him. "Why did you have to come over here right now?" she cried, fighting the urge to hug him.

Dro closed the distance between them, wrapping her in his arms. "Because I need you in my life. And I love you."

Their lips were drawn to each other's like magnets. Forever met his passion with her own desire, the lovers expressing how much they missed one another without the use of words.

When Dro's hands slipped down to her waist, he broke the kiss, face twisting in a frown.

"What?" Forever asked, searching his eyes.

He lifted the sweatshirt and began feeling her stomach. Surprise, confusion, and a thousand other unnamable emotions played across his face. When he tried to speak, the words wouldn't come out right. "Is. You. Why?"

Even though his words didn't make sense, Forever fully understood what he was trying to ask. "I tried to tell you a couple months ago, but you hung up on me."

The unnamed emotions continued to play across his features as he held a hand on her belly. "When did you find out? How far are you?"

"When I was in the hospital after we got shot. I'm four months. I think it happened when we went to North Dakota."

When the realization he was about to be a father again hit him, he hung his head, tears sliding from his eyes, a smile spreading across his face.

Forever couldn't see his reaction and thought he was mad. "I hope you're not mad I didn't tell you. I tried, but…."

She stopped talking when he lifted his head, showing tearstained eyes. Seeing him cry made her cry, and they wrapped arms around one another, holding on tight. The lovers didn't speak for a couple of moments, just stood near the front door, hugging and crying.

When their lips found each other's again, the passion was heightened times ten. They kissed their way to the nearest piece of furniture, clothes flying as they neared the couch. After they were naked, Dro sat on the couch, Forever standing before him. His face moved slowly toward her protruding belly, placing loving kisses. She cradled his head in her hands, the tender display of affection sending a chill through her body. Then he spun her around, searching her back for the bullet wounds. One was near her lower spine, the other on her right shoulder blade. He stood and placed kisses on both wounds before spinning her around again, finding her lips.

She lay on the couch, and he went down with her, spreading her legs and sliding in between. Their lovemaking was slow and passionate and beautiful. When he thrust inside of her, she pushed back, lifting her hips to meet him, wanting his all. Neither rushed. It wasn't about busting a nut or having an orgasm. They took their time, enjoying the feel of the one they loved giving from the deepest place inside their beings.

The climax was epic and satisfying, but neither had enough. When Dro sat up, she straddled his lap, kissing his lips, keeping her eyes open and staring at him while she rode. They continued riding the waves of lust, pleasure, and lovemaking until they were satisfied. Then they lay on the couch, their limbs intertwined, completeness filling their insides.

"Come with me to North Dakota," Forever said, staring deeply into his eyes, her heart's true desire showing in her pupils. "Let's raise our baby and get married. I love you. I need you. Please."

Instead of answering her, he asked a question. "Do you think God will forgive us of anything?"

She searched his eyes, trying to find the meaning behind the question. "Yes. The Bible says there is only one unpardonable sin. Why are you asking?"

He was silent for a moment. "I got a lotta blood on my hands."

Forever stared at him some more, searching and finding the answers in the darkness of his eyes. The truth scared her, making her look away. "Oh. Wow."

"I tried to kill his daughter."

That got Forever's attention, her voice squeaking from between her lips. "You killed a child?"

"Nah. I tried, but couldn't do it. I want that nigga so bad I can't think of nothing else. I heard everything you've been telling me about letting God take care of him, but I can't let this go. I want to be with you and the baby. I want to raise him or her and be yo' husband. But if I don't take care of this, I won't be able to live with myself."

Forever dropped her head, taking a moment to gather her words. "I don't want you to do it, but it sounds like I can't stop you. Is that when it's going to be over? After you kill him?"

He nodded.

"But I don't want to be with a murderer. I don't want you to go to prison. I want you to help me raise the baby. Don't you see God gave you another chance to be a father and raise your child?"

"I see that. But I gotta do what I gotta do. And I also gotta go to court in a couple days. I caught a gun charge."

Forever frowned. "When? Why are you just now telling me this?"

"I didn't wanna tell you before. I didn't know what was happening between us."

"So, how much time are you facing?"

"Ten years."

She shook her head and closed her eyes. When she opened them again, tears threatened to spill. "Ruben! How much trouble do you need to get into before you realize enough is enough?"

"I know. I thought about that. It's a lot I can't tell you right now. But just know I'm trynna make it out alive, and I'ma come back to you when I put this all behind me. I just need a little more time."

***

"Brandon said this gon' be over fast. He filing a motion to get the case thrown out," Dro explained to Crush as they walked the corridors of the Milwaukee County Courthouse.

"On what grounds?"

"I don't know. I think illegal search and seizure."

"Your neighbor called the police after the shootout with Tae, right?"

"Yeah. When he killed Scooter."

"I don't think the judge gon' grant that motion. Probable cause is the shooting."

Dro gave his uncle a look. "Damn, Crush. You sho know how to rain on a nigga parade."

Crush laughed. "My bad, nephew. I just didn't want you I to get your hopes too high and be let down."

"You did a good job shooting my balloon out the sky," Dro mumbled before walking through the big oak courtroom doors. He spotted Brandon waiting near the from row. A few rows behind him was a group of people that made him curse aloud.

"What the fuck?"

"You okay, Nephew?" Crush asked, looking around to find the cause of Dro's alarm.

"Nah. Forever here."

Crush followed Dro's line of sight. "Man, she looks way better in person. She so fine I'd put her dirty bath water in a little spray bottle and wear that shit like it was Gucci Cologne."

Dro ignored the comment, eyeing his unexpected supporters. Forever wasn't alone. Sasha, Stanley, and Pastor McClain had all shown up. After uncomfortable waves, he walked over to Brandon.

"Hey, Ruben. How are you feeling?"

"I'm okay."

"Good. This won't take long. I'm going to make an argument to get the case thrown out. The judge will most likely deny it, but we want it on the record in case we have to appeal. Lotta these judges are stupid as fuck, and they misquote the laws all the time. If he does, we might be able to use it against him later. I also wanna let the DA know we're fighting this. Might make them come with a deal that excludes you going to prison."

Like Brandon said, the hearing was over quickly. It only took fifteen minutes for the judge to deny the motion and proceed with setting a pretrial date for next month. When Dro walked into the spectator section, he was greeted by Forever's open arms.

"Hi, Ruben! We came to show our support. I wanted to make up for not being there for you after Asia's party."

"Thanks," he smiled before turning to the others. "Hey, Sasha. 'Sup, Stanley? Pastor McClain, this is a heck of a surprise."

The older man smiled heartily as they embraced. "Forever called and told me you were going through some tough times, and I wanted to show some support. Do you mind if we walk and talk?"

"Nah. Let's go." They walked from the courtroom followed by the entourage.

"I heard about the death of your daughter, and I want to offer my condolences. I can't even begin to imagine what that feels like," the pastor began. "And I also want to encourage you to find your way back to God. You haven't been in church in months, and I imagine you might be mad at God, questioning why He let this terrible thing happen. I've buried countless children and young people that died before they had the chance to experience life, and I've asked God that question after every funeral. There are some things only God has the answers to. You may not like hearing that, but that's the only answer He's given me. And it's okay to be mad. You've experienced a great loss. But what you shouldn't do is allow the death of your baby girl to create a spiritual death in you. Just because you don't understand the path you're on doesn't means He's not leading you. When life hits you, what's inside you will come out of you. This is why you read the Bible and come to church to get filled up with Jesus' living water. Faith don't stop the storm, son. It builds a shelter."

Chapter 16

"I ain't feeling this, Block. Why don't we do something else? Sam know me," America complained, adjusting the small, black halter top that barely covered her big-ass titties. She also wore a pair of little tan shorts that showed off her phatty.

"Do you love me or not? If you wanna fuck with me, this how we gon' get down. This shit easy. Do what I said and er'thang gon' be good. Quit all that whining," Block said, looking toward the food mart's door.

"But what if he call the police? I ain't trynna go to jail. Just let me do it my way. I can get the money."

"Bitch, do what the fuck I said!" Block exploded, slapping her across the face. "These mu'fuckas ain't callin' the police. What he gon' say? He got robbed trynna get his dick sucked? Quit being scared and go take care of that bidness. Daddy need to get right."

After getting slapped and snapped on, America knew not to argue. Block didn't play that shit and would beat her ass. Hoping to avoid another black eye, she climbed from the Camry and made the slow walk through the dark toward the mini-mart.

The front door was locked, so she had to knock and wait. A few moments later the owner appeared from the back room. He was an older Middle Eastern man named Sam. He had owned and operated the store for fifteen years.

"I'm closed," he said, waving her away.

"Wait! Sam, I just need to get something real quick. It won't take long. Please," America begged.

After a stare, he walked over and unlocked the door. "If you were anybody else, I wouldn't have let you in. What do you need?"

"Um, I just need a blunt and something to drink. Thank

you so much. I didn't feel like driving far this late at night."

"Come on in and get what you need so I can get home."

Sam followed her to the cooler, eyeing her bouncing backside. America had an ass made for twerking, and the shorts hugged it just right, no panty lines because she didn't like to wear underwear. She watched him in the security mirror and seen him checking her out. When he was hooked, she opened the cooler and bent over, poking her ass out. He didn't hide the fact he was checking her out.

"What you looking at?" she smiled.

He grinned from ear to ear. "Something very beautiful. My, my, my!"

She dropped it to the floor and brought it back up, teasing the old man. "I don't bite. Not that hard. Unless you want me to."

He closed the distance between them, slapping her ass, lust in his eyes. "I like to be bitten. You wanna bite?"

"I don't bite for free. Cost money for me to put my lips on you."

"Come to the back with me. Let's talk."

As they walked to the back of the store, America thought about telling him he forgot to lock the door. She didn't want to have anything to do with the robbery. But she also didn't want to piss off Block and lose her man and dope connection. Instead of thinking with common sense, stupidity kept her mouth closed.

"I don't got that much time. What do you want?" she asked when they were in the back.

He gripped her soft ass cheeks and felt her breasts. "I want you longer. Can you come back?"

"Not tonight. I got somebody waiting for me. I'll come back another time. You want some head?"

He nodded. "How much for a blow job?"

"Just fifty."

He pulled out a wad of cash, peeling off a hundred dollar bill. "Take this. Keep the change."

After stuffing the bill in her bra, she dropped to her knees and went to work. The old man was limp, but she had skills and got him hard quickly. She wanted to make him nut before Block came in. If it was possible, she hoped to get out with the hundred and not be party to the crime.

Sam lay back against the wall and closed his eyes, loving the feel of her full lips wrapped around his dick. A noise near the door made him look up. Block walked in the room wearing a surgical mask and holding the .357 Mag.

"Oh, yeah! Gettin' yo' dick sucked, huh? Where that safe at, old man?"

America screamed and lay on the floor.

Sam lifted his hands. "I already emptied it and took it to the bank. I don't have no money here."

Block slapped him in the face with the pistol, knocking the old man to the floor. "Lie to me again and I'ma bang yo' bitch-ass. Where the safe, bitch!"

"Okay! Okay! I'll take you. Please don't hit me," Sam pleaded, crawling to his knees.

Block grabbed him by the arm, forcing him to stand. They walked toward a makeshift closet at the back of the room. Inside was a three-foot safe. Sam put in the code and opened it. Block shoved him aside and reached for the money.

Figuring the old man wasn't a threat and needing to use both hands to stuff the money in his pockets, Block sat the gun atop the safe. He was so busy stuffing the loot that he didn't notice the old man going under the back of his shirt until it was too late.

"Shit!" Block cursed, grabbing his gun off the safe and ducking out of Sam's line of sight.

The old man pulled a small .380 Glock and started shooting. Block fired back blindly as he ran from the room, leaving America. The old man chased, firing wildly behind the fleeing robber. Knowing he only had three bullets and not wanting to test the old man's skill with the automatic, Block didn't even run for America's Camry. He just kept on running into the darkness, barely escaping the old man's fury.

America tried to run from the store but Sam wasn't having it.

"No you don't! Stop right there or I'll shoot your ass," he threatened, pointing the pistol.

America did the only thing she could do and began crying. "Please, Sam. Let me go. I didn't have nothing to do with this. I didn't know he was going to rob you."

***

After getting away from the scene unharmed, Block ran a few blocks over, ducking onto a side street. He was pissed he left his phone in America's car. He needed a ride. It was past midnight, and the streets were almost deserted. Which was good because it was easy to get away if he spotted the police.

Doing the only thing he could, Block found the nearest bus stop and waited in the darkness until the bus came. After a ten minute ride, he got off in a familiar North side neighborhood on Sherman and Center. Three blocks later, he walked up to a Victorian-styled house with chipped blue and white paint and balding grass out front.

After knocking on the door, he waited. "Who dat?" someone called from the other side of the door.

"Block. Let me in."

Locks clicked and the door opened. In the doorway stood a chubby, light-skinned nigga holding a black Mac-12. "Fuck you ain't call first, nigga?"

"I lost my phone," Block said, looking around nervously. "Let me in, Eddie."

Block's paranoia rubbed off on Eddie, making him look around. "Fuck wrong wit' chu, nigga?"

"I'm hot. I need to grab something and get the fuck off these streets."

Eddie stepped aside. "Yo' hot-ass bet' not brought no bullshit to my spot."

Inside the house was plush with carpeted floors, leather furniture, big screen with a PlayStation 3 hooked up. Two young hustlers were playing Call Of Duty while Dirty watched.

"This shit look real as fuck," Dirty laughed, the good weed he smoked making him feel like he was in the game.

"Let me get a gram, S-Dot," Block said, walking into the living room. The robbery made him twenty-five hundred dollars richer, and he couldn't wait to get the beige powder in his nose.

The young hustler was caught up in a battle and couldn't pause the game. "A'ight. Let me fuck these bitch-ass niggas up. Mu'fuckas tried to hit us."

"What you running from, bitch?" Eddie asked as he plopped down on the couch.

"I damn near killed a nigga. Robbed a store. I think my bitch got knocked."

S-Dot had just lost the video game gun battle, and hearing about a real one got his attention. "You talkin' 'bout that thick shorty I seen you with the other day?"

"Yeah. She America. A li'l down-ass bitch, too," he said regrettably.

"Betta get that bitch some bail money 'fore she tell on yo' fool-ass," Eddie laughed.

"I can't afford no bail. Her bitch-ass baby daddy prolly could, but I know Dro ain't gon' get that bitch out. I'ma just have to go on the run, 'cause I ain't goin' to jail."

Eddie and Dirty looked at each other at the same time.

"Dro is yo' bitch baby daddy? The Savage nigga?" Eddie asked.

"Yeah. I had to put my hands on that fuck-boy a li'l while back. Bitch-ass nigga."

"You know where that nigga live?" Dirty asked.

Block seen the intense interest in Dro and planned to use it to his advantage. "What's goin' on wit' you niggas and Dro?"

Dirty started as if he was about to get up from the couch, his expression serious. "Do you know where that nigga lay his head at?"

"Nah. But I know the li'l bitch house he be going by. That's where I beat his ass at. He owns some laundromats, too."

"Show me where she live at right now and I'ma give you two grams," Eddie said.

The ride to Shamika's house only took five minutes. During the ride, Block sat in the back seat of Eddie's Benz and got high.

"You sure this is it?" Dirty asked as he stared up at the house. The lights were off and it was pitch black.

"Yeah, that's it. Shamika and America used to be friends," Block nodded, eyes glossy and red.

Dirty nodded to Eddie.

"A'ight. Where you say you wanna go?"

"Take me on Twenty-Sixth and Center. I gotta get the fuck off these streets."

The ride was silent, Meek Mill rapping from the car

speakers. When the Benz turned onto Twenty-Sixth and Center, Eddie killed the lights and drove down an alley. After parking next to a garage, he tapped Block on the leg to wake him. The diesel had him nodding.

"This yo' spot."

"Okay. Good looking. Once I get another phone, I'ma get at you."

Block looked around as he climbed from the back seat, being cautious. Dirty got out with him, putting the 40 Glock in his face and squeezing the trigger.

Pop!

When Block fell to the ground, Dirty gave him two more in the head.

"You didn't have to do 'im like that," Eddie said as he sped toward the alley exit.

"That nigga was cooked, li'l cuz. That bitch gon' tell on him, and he was prolly gon' tell on us or S-Dot trynna make a deal. Fuck that nigga."

***

"Twenty, what it do, nigga?"

"Dro, could you come bail me out?" America asked.

Hearing his baby mamma's voice surprised the hell out of him. "Why the fuck you calling my phone from jail? I thought you was Twenty."

"Block's bitch-ass robbed Sam and left me. I been locked up three days. Can you pay my bail and come get me out?"

The question surprised him and pissed him off. "I don't fuck with you like that. Don't call my phone no more." He ended the call.

"Who was that?" Crush asked, hearing the anger in Dro's voice.

"America. Her and her nigga pulled a move and she got knocked. Asking me to come bail her out," he answered, pulling up to a red stop light.

"How much is the bail?"

"I don't know. Bitch got some nuts callin' me. I shoulda blew her brains out for getting me locked up. Karma is a bitch."

"A fine-ass bitch, too," Crush laughed.

After pulling into the underground garage and finding a parking spot, the pair hopped the elevator and rode to Whisper's floor. Tocorra's fine ass answered the door.

"Who is the niggas?" Dro asked as soon as he walked in the condo.

Lunatic held out a tablet, a serious look on his face. "Here they go. They was at the party. I think the whole thing was a setup."

Dro grabbed the tablet and sat down. Crush sat close. "What is we looking at?"

"This the club footage. The nigga Eddie is at the table talking to Whisper. Me and Twenty at the bar. The bitch that set him up is in the red dress. She was talking to the nigga in the blue T-shirt before we got there, and they left together."

Dro looked to Whisper. "Who the fuck is Eddie?"

"Nigga used to fuck with Monster. I knew the nigga looked familiar, but I couldn't figure out why when we was at the party. But I knew it was gon' come to me."

"Who is the nigga in the blue shirt?"

"I don't know, but he connected to the female, so he connected to Eddie."

"We know where they at?"

"They got a spot over on Center," Whisper grinned. "We got the advantage 'cause they don't know we figured it out. Hit them niggas hard and get them numbers off y'all heads."

Dro looked to Lunatic. "You riding?"

He pulled a Taurus from underneath a couch pillow. "Hell yeah! How you wanna go in?"

"Leave that to me," Crush spoke up."

***

"What you see in there, baby?" Crush asked.

The emaciated and disheveled woman slipped into the back seat of the rental car, smiling like she had cracked a mind-bending code. "Four of 'em. Eddie is in there. S-Dot, Freddie Mac, and Dirty is the one in the video with the blue shirt," April answered.

Dro pulled away from the curb, driving the Regal off into the night. His finger was itching to squeeze a trigger and get back for Twenty. "How long you say before you coming back?"

"Thirty minutes, like you said. Y'all can drop me off back at the house. I can keep this, right?" she asked, not wanting to give up the gram of heroin.

"That's you, baby," Crush affirmed. "But you can make one more if you go back and get 'em to open the door and let us in. It's up to you."

She looked toward the front of the car at the backs of Dro and Lunatic's heads, then back at Crush. "I don't gotta go in no more?"

"Nah, baby. Just knock on the door. Once they open it, you can run. Or you can just take what you got and leave. It's up to you."

She stared into Crush's eyes, trying to read him, hoping he was telling the truth. "Okay. I'ma do it. Damn, Crush. You look good all cleaned up. Seeing you make me wanna go fuck up a McDonald's and go to jail. You came out looking good."

"I suggest you do it. Ain't no sense in being in that house with Earl and them dying slow. I can get you somewhere to stay whenever you ready."

She could see the concern for her welfare in her ex-boyfriend's eyes. "Thanks, Crush. I ain't ready yet. But when I am, I'ma call you."

Thirty minutes later, April was back on the porch of Eddie's bando. She had already knocked, waiting for the door to open. Dro stood off to one side of the door holding a 40. Crush was next to him with a .38 Special. Lunatic was on the other side with the 9 Taurus. All of them wore black, trying to blend in with the night.

"Who dat?"

"It's April," she said, nodding to Crush, signaling she was about to run away.

Crush shook his head no, keeping her in place. The locks began clicking on the door. As soon as it opened, Dro's pistol was up and ready. Eddie had a .9 mil in his hand, but wasn't expecting to be staring down the barrel of a pistol. He did the only thing he could do.

Blinked.

Bocca, bocca, bocca!

All the bullets hit the mark in the face. The last thing Eddie remembered before he died was the feet of the Savages stepping over his body.

Crush grabbed April and forced her into the house as well.

When Dirty heard the shooting, his instincts kicked in immediately, and he didn't hesitate to grab the Mac-12 off the table. S-Dot and Freddie Mac froze, unsure how to react. That indecision cost them their lives as the Savages began blazing.

Dirty backtracked toward the bedroom, letting the Mac-

12's 45-caliber bullets tear up and shred everything they hit. Dro and Lunatic barely had time to get out of the way as the Mac spit rapid-fire. Then all went silent.

Dro nodded to his nigga. Luna understood, and they crept silently toward the room door. Dirty must've sensed them getting close, because he started shooting again. Wood splintered as the door was shredded. The Savages had to take cover, neither of them wanting to get hit by the slugs.

Realizing they we weren't going to get past the door without at least one of them being shot, Lunatic shook his head, calling off the hit. They backpedaled toward the front door and let their pistols ride, hoping to hit Dirty with a stray.

When Crush seen his boys coming toward the foyer, he put the revolver to the back of April's head.

"Sorry, baby. Can't leave no witnesses."

Pop!

J-Blunt

Chapter 17

"Is you my nigga, Dro? What are we doing?" Shamika asked, kissing him on the neck. They had just finished fucking. He was laid back in bed, smoking a blunt. Shamika was wrapped around him, unable to keep her hands and lips to herself.

"We doing us. What you mean? I fuck with you the long way."

"Could we be more than that?" she asked, sucking his nipple. "I'm feeling you, baby, and I wanna know if you feel the same way."

He paused a moment to think. "Because I fuck with you, I ain't gon' lie to you. I'ma give you the truth, and you decide what to do with it. Forever pregnant. She got my heart. Whenever I get all this bullshit behind me, we leaving Milwaukee. I like you and fuck with you, but I can't be nothing more than yo' friend, baby. Real shit."

A flicker of disappointment flashed in her eyes. "Damn. I really like yo' ass, nigga. I appreciate you not lying to me. Most niggas would. You a real nigga, and I respect you. I hope you and Forever work out. And if it don't, you know where I live. Door always open."

"Only thing I know how to be is me. A real nigga," he chuckled before passing her the blunt. "Oh yeah, yo' girl called me last night from jail."

"Who is my girl?" she frowned.

"America. Her and Block robbed somebody, and he left her. I think she got charged. Wanted me to bail her ho-ass out. I wouldn't piss on that bitch if she was on fire."

"On what she locked up?"

"I'm for real. Her stupid ass got what she had coming."

"Damn, Dro. I feel kinda bad for my girl. Even though we ain't on the same level no more, I still got love for her ass.

I don't want her to go to jail. That nigga fucked up her life."

"Fuck her and that nigga. They deserve each other."

***

After lying around and fucking Shamika all over the house, Dro went out to check on the laundromats and Crush. Activity had picked up at both sites, and things were starting look up.

During the drive, he got a call. It was Forever.

"Hey, baby," he answered.

"Why didn't you call me at lunch like you said you would?"

Dro thought about what he was doing at 11 o'clock that morning. Shamika might've been on the kitchen table getting drilled from the back. "I slept late. What you doing?"

"Nothing. I just got home. You didn't forget about the doctor's appointment, did you?"

"Nah. What makes you think I would forget? You think I'm a scumbag?"

"No. I know you'll be there. I was just reminding you. I can't wait to see you. Being away from you is hard. I already found a house in Bismarck. Two bedrooms."

The thought of a peaceful life with his girl and baby tucked away safely in another state made him smile. "I can't wait to be with you, too. You know I'm staying away to keep you safe. I don't want nothing to happen to you and the baby."

"Yeah. I know you love us. I'm just ready to get to a normal life with you. Want to wake up next to you so bad, you don't even know."

Dro kicked it with his girl on the way to the laundromat. After ending the call, he hit up Crush, but got no answer. He went in the laundromat and checked the utility room.

Sometimes Crush had to fix things, and he wanted to check downstairs before going up. When he didn't find him, he climbed the stairs to the apartment.

Crush was sitting on the couch, reflecting a desperate look. On the table in front of him was a drug kit, along with heroin and a syringe.

"The fuck you doing, Crush!" Dro snapped, grabbing the drugs.

Crush looked sober, his eyes clear. "I didn't do it. If you'da came through that door a minute later, I was gon' be nodding off on this couch. It's hard being alone, Nephew. I think that was the reason I stayed in that nasty-ass house with all those people. And I feel bad about April, too. I cared about her, Nephew. At night, my mind be playing tricks on me. I need to be back with Candice and my daughter."

Dro felt sympathy for his uncle's situation. Crush was a good dude and needed to succeed, but he was vulnerable and needed the love and support of loved ones to bring him through the rough times.

Dro pocketed the pack and sat next to him. "Damn, my nigga. I know this shit hard, but you can't go back to that shit. What about Sandra? Y'all been together a couple months. Why don't you try to get her to move in."

"I like Sandra. She's fun and pretty, but she can't fill that spot, Nephew. Believe me, I wanted her to. Only one body fit next to mine."

"Okay, man. I got you, Unc. You staying with me at all times. We sleeping at Shamika's house. I'll be yo' rock, my nigga. You can't go back to shooting that bullshit."

The men shared an embrace, the love and loyalty real. They were blood. They shared a bond through Dro's father that was unbreakable.

The vibrating of Dro's phone got his attention. It was a

jail call. "What's good, brah?"

"This America. Can we talk?"

"Bitch, I thought I told you not to call my phone no more."

"Wait. Please don't hang up. Just gimme one minute to say what I need to say."

He didn't know why he wanted to hear her out. "What you gotta say? You got one minute."

"Not one minute literally. Let's talk."

"You got fifty-five seconds. Time running."

"What? Okay. I'm sorry for calling the police. It was Block. He took over my life and used to beat my ass if I didn't listen."

That defense had me tripping.

"We been through too much together. Our baby died," she got choked up. "And it changed me. I blamed you. I was mad at you, and I hated you. I'm sorry."

There was genuine sincerity in her voice. She was really sorry. And even if he never admitted it, he appreciated hearing the apology for the heavy burden and accusation. "A'ight. I'ma forgive you for that shit. Asia dying changed me, too. Don't come at me with no bullshit no more. I ain't playing."

"I won't. Can you pay my bail and get me the fuck outta here? It's twenty-five thousand. I can't do this jail shit."

"I can't do that, America. You on yo' own with that shit. I forgive you, but I ain't fucking with you. You put me in jail. You need a three-way?"

"Ruben, you really about to do me like that? You gon' leave me in here?"

"Yeah. You did that shit. Tell Deidra to bail you out. Yo' Momma can put up the house."

"She won't do it. We got into it."

"I don't know what to tell you."

"What about that bogeyman?"

He frowned. "What the fuck you talking about?"

"That bogeyman and his kids. I seen it on TV."

The sting of betrayal stabbed Dro in the heart. She was trying to set him up. Fire began burning through his chest.

"You tripping. I'ma try to get you a care package. I got something to do. Call me later."

"What was that about?" Crush asked when he seen the look on his face.

"That was America. She tried to set me up. Asked me about Monster on the phone."

Crush's eyes popped like he took a bump of coke. "Shit, man! Them calls recorded. She didn't really do that, did she?"

"Yeah. 'Cause I wouldn't bail her out."

"You know what you gotta do, right?"

"Hell yeah. I gotta bail her ass out!"

***

Deidra sat in her Dodge Caravan outside the county jail waiting for her daughter to he released. She had been waiting for a hour and expected her out at any moment. And she couldn't wait to bust her daughter's ass for allowing a nigga to fuck her life up. Deidra had taught her better, gave her the scoop on men and the games they play.

Just when she thought she was about to burst from the pent-up anger and emotions, America stepped from the building. Deidra's heart skipped as she hit the horn. Even though she was mad, she was happy to see her daughter free.

"Hey, Momma! I missed you so much," America cried, hugging her mother after climbing in the van.

"I missed you, too, baby. And I'm mad. How the fuck you let a nigga get you this fucked up? You don't let no nigga tear you down," the mother lectured.

"I know, Momma. I was messed up. Losing Asia hurt. I think I might need to go to counseling."

"No, you don't need no counseling. That's for white people. You a strong, black queen. Betta put yo' shoulders back and lift yo' chin. You a woman. A black woman, at that. We been through worse. You gon' make it, and I'ma make sure of that. Somebody put the money in my mailbox to get you out, and we gon' take it from here. And you betta stay away from Block's no-good ass. He the reason you in this."

"Fuck Block. I told them it was all his fault. I'm not going down for him."

After spending the day getting lectured and loved by her mother, America went home. She didn't make it in the house 'til after ten, and she was tired. After a week in jail showering with nasty soap and sleeping on a paper-thin mattress, she couldn't wait to take a bath and sleep in a real bed. Her bed.

She took her time bathing, allowing the water to wash away all the bullshit she endured in the last week. One thing was for sure: she was done with Block's no-good ass. He left her to die or go to jail.

She had just gotten out of the bath when there was a knock on the door. The thought of Block being outside sent a shiver down her spine. She wished she had one of Dro's guns in the house as she wrapped a towel around her body and went to answer the door.

"Who is it?"

"Dro."

Surprise filled her being at the sound of his voice. She knew he dropped the money in the mailbox. The forgiveness was real.

She snatched open the door, happy to see him. "Thank you for getting me out. Thank you so much, Dro!" she sang, wrapping him in a hug.

"You know I got you. Let me in real quick."

She let him go and allowed him in the house. After closing the door, she spun, noticing the pained look on his face. "What's wrong."

"You was really gon' do me like that?" The emotion in his eyes was strong. The betrayal was devastating.

"No, Dro. I just heard it around the jail that Savages tore shit up. I didn't know you was out there like that."

"I just wanted to look in yo' eyes, America, so I can always remember what betrayal looks like. I used to do everything for you. You was my nigga. Wasn't nothing I wouldn'ta done for you."

America got teary-eyed. "Dro, it wasn't like that, baby. I wasn't gon' –"

The pistol in his hand made her stop speaking.

"This don't take away nothing we shared. I'm about to have a baby, and I can't let you take me away from my family."

Pop!

The bullet to the forehead didn't kill America. Dro thought she died before he shot her, right when she realized he was about to kill her.

J-Blunt

Chapter 18

"Man, Dro. Shit ain't gon' be the same without you, my nigga. Damn, I wish you niggas could come to the ATL with us. We would fuck the city up, my nigga," Lunatic said, feeling like he was losing his brothers. They were in Dro's Charger, driving toward Whisper's condo. They had just come from selling Lunatic's car to a dealership.

"Sun don't shine forever, my nigga," Dro said, taking a drink from the bottle of Remey. "We gotta walk away while we still can. While niggas still got the opportunity. We did it all and seen it all in the streets. Now it's time to see what the good life got ta offer. As soon as I put this shit with J-Mac behind, I'm moving to North Dakota with Forever."

"I hear you, my nigga. I'm just glad we get the opportunity to make these moves. Tae ain't gon' get the chance, and it ain't looking good for Twenty. You 'bout to have another baby. Got the laundromats. I'm finna put my hand in this pimp shit. Damn, Dro. We got crazy-ass life stories, my nigga. If we wrote books about our lives, them bitches would be bestsellers."

Dro smiled. "Real shit. Hopefully this shit with Monster over. I wish we coulda got Dirty, but I think we sent a message. I'ma remember that nigga, though. If I get the opportunity, I'ma knock his shit back before I hit it."

"I regret not gettin' his bitch-ass, too. Them niggas prolly the niggas that killed Tae. I wanted him so bad. But he had something fat, and I wasn't taking no chances goin' in that room."

"Me either," Dro chuckled, the men becoming quite.

"You got any regrets? I know we did a lot of shit, but I regret some of it."

Dro thought about killing Tae and America. "Yeah. A

couple."

"I regret poppin' Trell sister. I didn't have to do it, but I had to show that nigga I don't fuck around," Lunatic confessed.

Dro thought about the incident. Trell had been an associate of the Savages, and he also became their enemy when he got mad at Lunatic for fucking his bitch. Shot at Lunatic and then fled town. Because he couldn't get to him, Lunatic shot his sister.

"Yeah, that was fucked up. Shonda was kinda cool."

"What you regret?"

Dro let out a breath. "I had to bang America last night."

Lunatic laughed. "Quit bullshitting, nigga. I'm on some real shit right now."

Dro took his eyes off the road to look at his boy. "I ain't bullshitting. She tried to get me to talk about killing Monster on the phone while she was in jail. Bitch was gon' set me up if I didn't pay her bail. So, I bailed her out last night and killed her."

Lunatic looked stunned. "Damn. That bitch was trynna put you under the jail like that? After doing that shit with the car, you would think she learned. I don't feel no sympathy. And I don't think you should, either. Bitch tried to get on some rat-shit."

"I know. But I used to love her, my nigga. We had a shorty. I didn't wanna do it, but I had to protect my family. Couldn't let her take me away from my new baby."

"You don't gotta explain it to me, my nigga. I understand. I ain't letting nobody testify on me if I can do something about it. Fuck that."

"I regret Tae, too."

"Yeah, I wish you niggas wouldn'ta had that fight, either. I regret not stopping it before it happened."

"I ain't talking about the fight."

Lunatic looked over at him. "Fuck you talking about?"

Dro couldn't say the words. And he didn't have to. The devastation on Lunatic's face told he'd figured it out. "You killed Tae?"

"I couldn't let it go, brah."

Lunatic just stared at him, a jumble of emotions passing across his features. Then he repeated himself, like he couldn't believe the first response. "You killed Tae?"

Dro nodded. "I had to. He tried to kill me in my own house and shot my dog. That was the only thing I had connecting me to my baby. And I'm fighting a gun charge because of that shit. He did too much. I couldn't let it go. I just wish it wouldn't have got that far. My head was so fucked up after that nigga killed my baby that I wasn't accepting no bullshit from nobody. I shouldn't have put my hands on him. I created that whole situation, and I regret that."

Lunatic's face was crestfallen, like he just heard his entire family died. He turned to look out the windshield, unable to look at Dro. "Damn, fam. I wish you wouldn't've told me that shit. You shoulda let me believe them other niggas did it."

Dro didn't have a response. Nothing he said would take away how Lunatic felt, so they rode without speaking the rest of the way to the condo.

After parking in the underground garage, they continued in silence until Lunatic spoke.

"Tell me how it happened."

"You sure you wanna hear it?"

"Tell me, Dro. I gotta know how my nigga went out."

"I followed Twenty to the house and lamped on him. Learned when o'girl got off work and used her to get in. The nigga was ready and shot first. Killed her. I caught 'im by the back door. He tried to cop a plea, but I didn't wanna hear it.

Stood over him and did it."

Lunatic hung his head and nodded. "A'ight. I don't got no words right now, brah. Shit just fucked up. I'ma get up wit' chu later. Stay dangerous."

"You already know. Savage."

During the drive to Shamika's house, Dro went back and forth about whether or not he should have told Lunatic he offed Tae. The pain reflected was real, and Dro hated that he caused it. But he was getting back to who he was and wanted to be honest with his boy. And he would have to do the same thing with Twenty. However they took it was on them. He didn't want to hide shit from his niggas.

When he got to Shamika's house, she was walking out the front door. "Where you going looking like that?" he asked, checking her out. Her body looked crazy good in the heels, pink leggings, and a half-halter top.

"Got a bachelor party. I'ma be back in a couple hours. What you about to do?"

"Shit. Chill here. Where Crush?"

"He left a li'l while ago. Said he was going to the laundromat. See you later, baby."

Dro slapped her on the ass, watching it jiggle. "Stay sexy."

She smiled over her shoulder, throwing on the Prada shades. "I don't know how to do nothing else, baby."

***

The full moon sat high in the sky, shining down on the entrance of Red's Cafe like a spotlight. Crush stood near the restaurant's parking lot, close enough to see who was coming out, but remaining far enough so as not to be seen. He'd been waiting for five minutes. *Any minute now*, he thought.

At 10:07 he got his wish. From the glass double doors

emerged an older, fair-skinned, bald black man. He wasn't an imposing man, only stood about five-foot-seven with a slim build and wore a white chef uniform. He moved toward the gray Chevy Impala like a man tired from a long day's work.

"Billy!"

The chef spun around at the sound of his name, eyeing Crush as he approached. "Do I know you?"

Crush extended a hand. "I'm Chris. Savannah and Kathy's father."

Recognition shown in Billy's face as the men shook hands. "Oh. Hey, man. I couldn't see you in the dark. How's it going?"

"I'm just taking it one day at a time. Can I ride with you? I wanted to talk."

Suspicion shown in Billy's eyes. "How'd you know I worked here? What's going on?"

Crush lifted his hands in a peaceful gesture, palms out. "I come in peace, brother. I spoke to Candice, and she told me where you worked. I don't want any trouble. I just want to ride with you and talk."

After a brief stare, Billy nodded toward the passenger seat. "Get in."

When they were situated in the car, he wanted to know the nature of the visit. "So, what's so important that you had to come to my job to talk to me about it?"

"I wanted to talk to you about Candice."

Billy glanced over. "Why do you want to talk about my woman?"

"If you don't mind, I got dropped off. I'll pay you twenty for gas if you head toward Capitol."

"Keep the money. It's on the way home. Why do you want to talk about Candice? She's okay, right?" he asked as he pulled out of the parking lot.

"Yeah, she's fine. I've been out of their lives for a while, and now that I'm back, I want to know more about the new man. I'm sure you know my story from Candice and the girls, but I don't know yours. We haven't had the opportunity to sit down, and I was hoping we could take this opportunity to get to know each other better."

"I'll be honest, Chris. I don't know much about you. Just that you were into drugs. Candice and I rarely spoke about you."

Crush nodded, not knowing if Billy took a shot at him. "That's why I'm here. I just wanted you to know I love my girls. When I got rid of the drugs, I planned on coming home to them. But when I got there, I learned about you. Candice loves you, man. That was difficult to hear. She's a good woman. I took her through hell, and I regret it every day. I don't mean to pry, but I just want to know if you feel the same way about her that she feels about you?"

Billy thought for a moment. "I'll be honest, Chris, I've never loved a woman as much as I love Candice. Like you said, she is a good woman. Although I've only known her for a year and a half, the things we've been through during this time made us close. Losing Savannah was…. Well, you already know."

Hearing the love for Candice in his voice and the fact he was there to comfort Candice when Savannah died lit a fire inside Crush's chest. "Do you plan to marry her?"

"I'm not sure. We've discussed it, but I don't know if it's for us. I love her, and she loves me. I think that's all that matters right now."

"Do you have dreams?"

Billy looked at him strangely. "What kinda question is that?"

"It's an honest one. Do you have business plans?

Something you want to accomplish? Goals?"

Billy laughed. "Man, I'm not sure where this is going, but yeah. I dream. I used to want to open my own restaurant. I'm a chef."

Crush nodded. "I hear you, man. What if I helped you fund that dream and turn it into a reality?"

Billy gave him another look. "What's going on, Chris? Why would you do that for me?"

"This is the thing, man. I love Candice and my daughter. I lost a lot of time with them when I was out in the street getting high. I don't want to miss anything else. Candice is the love of my life, and I want her back. I'll give you fifty thousand dollars right now to walk away ."

Billy looked over and seen the seriousness in Crush's eyes. "Wow, man! Fifty thousand cash? You have that kind of money?"

"Yeah, I do. Damn near all the money I have. But I'll give it to you. Everything I got, you can have. Just let me have my girls back."

Billy was silent. Thinking. He had never been presented with such an offer. It almost sounded too good to be true. Fifty thousand dollars cash. He could start that restaurant and try to live out his dreams. But what about Candice? The love they shared was real. He wanted to spend the rest of his life with her. But starting a business was a once-in-a-lifetime opportunity. "I don't know, Chris. I don't want to hurt Candice. I love her, and she's a good woman."

Crush looked desperate. "Don't worry 'bout hurting her. I'll pick up those pieces. Worry about your business, getting that dream turned into real life."

Billy was silent again, thinking. "That's a good offer, man, and had it been any other woman, I would've accepted. But I can't. She's a good woman, worth more than money. I love her. I'm staying."

"I feel the same way. If you really love her, do what's best. Let me have my family back. Take the money and walk."

"I'm sorry, Chris. I can't walk away," Billy said, pulling up to a stoplight.

"There can't be two of us," Crush sighed, pulling the .357 from his pocket and shooting Billy in the face.

Pop! Pop!

***

"Where you been?" Dro asked when Crush walked through the front door.

"I was out checking the laundromats."

Dro looked him over suspiciously. "I went by the laundromats. I was looking for you. Why didn't you answer the phone? I called and texted."

"I had my phone off. What's up?"

Dro got up from the couch to get a closer look at his uncle, checking for signs of drug use. The old man looked calm, his eyes clear. "You been out fucking with that shit?"

"C'mon, Nephew. You know I know better. I was really at the laundromat. I'm good."

After another long stare, Dro sat back on the couch. "A'ight. Everything good?"

"Yeah. Never been better. Hold on," he said before pulling out his phone. "I just got a text from Kathy. Let me call her back real quick."

"Handle your business."

Crush dialed Kathy's number. She answered almost immediately. "Hey, baby. How you doing?" he asked before she started speaking in a rush. "Wait! Slow down. I can't hear you. What happened?"

Dro heard the change in Crush's tone and seen the serious look on his face. "What's goin' on, Unc?"

He lifted a finger, signaling Dro to hold on while he listened. "What happened to Billy? Are you sure? Okay. I'm on my way. Are you at home? Okay. I'm on my way."

"What happened to Billy?" Dro asked.

"Kathy said he got shot. Can you take me over there? I need to be with them."

Dro eyed his uncle for a moment. "You murked Billy?"

Crush looked away, shame keeping him from meeting his nephew's gaze. "When you really love somebody, you'll do anything for them."

J-Blunt

Chapter 19

"Good morning, Forever. How are you doing?" the doctor asked, extending a hand. Gweneth Emerson was a highly-decorated OBGYN. She ran her own private healthcare facility catering to black mothers.

"Fine. Ready for the checkup. This is my boyfriend, Ruben."

"How are you?" Dro asked, shaking her hand.

"I'm good," she said, looking the couple over. "You guys are really cute. Your baby is going to be beautiful."

"Thank you," Forever beamed, eating up the compliment.

"You're welcome. Well, let's get this started. Have a seat on the table. How are you eating? Are you taking the prenatal pills?"

The appointment only took twenty minutes. After determining she and the baby were healthy, they were on their way. Dro and Forever walked out of the clinic hand-in-hand, looking like a couple in love. His girl glowed with happiness, and he loved seeing the smile on her face.

When they stopped at her truck, he pulled out his phone. "Stop. Let me take a picture."

She leaned against the SUV and struck a pose.

"Yeah. Just like that. Now bend over and put it on that glass."

She took a swing at him. "You better stop playing with me. I'm not one of those strippers you used to deal with."

He laughed, closing the distance between them. "I know. I'm just playing. But it ain't nothing wrong with you being a stripper for yo' man."

"And it ain't nothing wrong with you being a stripper for your girl," she said, pecking him on the lips.

The lip-lock quickly went from a peck to a passionate

make-out. For a moment, they forgot they were in the parking lot of a health clinic.

"Oh, my God! You do something to me," Forever panted. "Come back to my house with me. Spend the rest of the day making love to me. I'm so turned on right now."

"Shit, you ain't said nothing. Let's go," he said, kissing her one more time before they hopped in their vehicles.

Dro had been trailing her for a couple minutes when he got a phone call. He checked the number on the screen, all thoughts of sex with his girl vanishing. "What up, Snake?"

"What's hangin', Dro? I found that package you was asking about."

Visions of executing J-Mac played through his mind. "I'm listening."

"This took a li'l time and was hard for me to get. Can't let this go for free."

"What is you playing around for, Snake? Say what you need to say."

He laughed. "I like you, Dro. You don't fuck around. Just gimme ten and he all yours."

"I'ma get wit' Whisper and have him wire it to you. Text me the info."

"You got it, boss. Happy hunting."

When the phone vibrated again, Dro took his eyes off the road to glance at the address. Powerful emotions waged a war inside him as he envisioned ending the revenge-fueled path he'd been on since his daughter died. Sex with his girl would have to wait a little longer. He reluctantly called Forever.

"You calling to tell me what song you wanna dance to?" Forever laughed.

When he heard the excitement in her voice, it pained him a little that he would have to upset her. "I'm sorry, baby. I gotta turn around. Something just came up. I gotta take care of this."

"Ruben, no!" she whined. "I haven't seen you in so long. Don't go. Please."

"Forever, you know I want to be with you. Trust me, this is important. Let me take care of this and I will be yours for the rest of our lives."

***

J-Mac sat on the couch, blowing out a cloud of smoke and watching it evaporate. The last couple months of his life had been hectic. The State Fair shooting was on all the news channels, and the reward for information leading to his arrest was more than one hundred thousand dollars. He had also made the FBI's most wanted list. It was only a matter of time before someone cashed in and sent the feds to kick in the door. That's why he constantly moved from house to house, city to city. Today it was Peoria, Illinois. Next week it would be somewhere else. Where that place was, he wasn't sure. All the locations had been secured by his OG, Rated-R.

As he sat on the couch smoking, he thought about his family. His momma, daddy, brother, and baby mamma had all been killed in cold blood. He knew it was the Savages. How they found his people was a mystery – one he would get to the bottom of when he put all the heat behind him. And he would kill all the Savages and everyone they knew.

"Them stripper hos on the way. They text said they down the street," Grizzly said, plopping down on the couch across from J-Mac.

"'Bout time. And they betta be bad. Niggas bet not be sending no more weak-ass hos through here. I don't fuck weak bitches."

"If we don't find another spot to lay low, we ain't gon'

have to worry 'bout gettin' pussy. Them feds don't fuck around. We gotta move again."

"Rated-R said he taking care of it, didn't he? He been wit' us this far. He ain't gon' fall off now."

"Nigga bet not. Not after all the work we put in on that deck. We made that block. Niggas respect the set because of some of the shit I did," Grizzly said.

A knock on the door made the goons halt their convo. J-Mac grabbed the Draco that was on the couch next to him.

"You ready, nigga?" Grizzly said, pulling a Desert Eagle and walking to the door.

"I stay ready so I won't have to get ready. Get the door."

"Who dat?" Grizzly asked, checking the peephole. Two females stood on the porch wearing ho clothes.

"Sayara and Star," they called.

Grizzly nodded to J-Mac, lowering the pistol. "We good." He said before opening the door. "What's up, y'all? Come in. I'm Grizzly."

"Hey, Grizzly!" They sang,

When the women walked in the house, he took a peek outside to check the scene. After deciding the coast was clear, he turned to close the door. And that's when he thought he seen something move near a parked car. He turned a half-second too slow, and the last thing he remembered seeing was a spark of fire.

Bocca, bocca, bocca, bocca, bocca, bocca, bocca!

Dro led the charge from behind the parked car, his 40s spitting rapid fire as him and Crush charged the porch. The nigga standing in the doorway jerked as slugs tore into his head and chest as he fell.

Dro didn't think twice about rushing inside the house, and the lack of caution almost cost his life.

Prrraaaattttt! Prrraaaattttt!

J-Mac let the Draco ride. Refusing to go out like Grizzly, he moved toward the back door, letting the chopper bullets fly. Dro was barely able to dodge the barrage of bullets, using the dancers for human shields. Metal cartridges dug into the flesh of the terrified strippers who didn't duck fast enough.

When the shooting stopped, he ran toward the back of the house just as J-Mac opened the door.

Bocca, bocca, bocca, bocca, bocca! The 40 spat.

Prrraaaattttt! J-Mac returned fire as he sprinted from the house into the backyard.

Boom, boom, boom!

The unmistakable explosions from the .44 Magnum let Dro know Crush was involved in the gun fight. And when he stepped into the backyard, he seen the damage. J-Mac was sprawled out on the ground, limbs twisted like a pretzel. The .44 bullets had taken chunks from his back. But he was still alive.

Dro and Crush reached him at the same time. Standing over him with their guns pointed at his face, both men squeezed the triggers until J-Mac's face was gone.

***

"I did it, baby," Dro cried, wiping the tears before they could spill from his eyes as he stared down at Asia's headstone. It felt like a burden had been lifted from his shoulders, and he finally felt a sense of justice for what happened to his baby. "I got that bitch-ass nigga. I'm sorry I couldn't protect you. But you about to have a brother or sister, and I promise you I will protect them with every breath in my body. Watch over us. I love you and I miss you, baby."

From the graveyard, he drove to Forever's house, not caring if he was being followed. Not caring if there was still a price on his head. It was done. He was leaving the city. He was ready for a new life. Ready to be with his woman and raise their baby. Ready for change.

After parking, he called Forever's phone.

"Are you okay?" she answered, sounding half asleep.

"I'm good. Come open the door."

"Ruben, it's three o'clock in the morning. Why are you calling so late."

"Because I'm outside. Open the door," he said before hanging up.

When he walked in the building, Forever was just opening the door. She wore one of his t-shirts, looking pissed off and half asleep. Dro didn't care. He walked in the apartment, slamming the door behind him, and wrapping her in his arms. She tried to protest, but he silenced her with a kiss, pawing at her body like a hungry animal attacking prey.

"Wait, Ruben! Let me lock the door."

"Fuck that door," he said, picking her up and carrying her to the bedroom. After dropping her on the bed, he thought about the unlocked door and went to lock it. He couldn't make it that easy for his enemies.

"What's going on?" Forever asked when he walked back in the room.

"I'm done. It's over," he said, pulling off his clothes.

Her eyes popped. "Are you serious? Is it really over?"

"Yeah. We can move tomorrow. But I don't wanna talk about it now. Take that shirt off. Yo' ass is mines!"

Forever snatched the shirt off and Dro dove on top of her like he was belly flopping into a swimming pool. Their kisses were sloppy and aggressive. He licked and kissed his way down her neck, stopping at her swelling breasts, sucking and teasing her nipples.

"Ooh, baby!" Forever moaned, rubbing his head.

After having his fill, he kissed her body some more, leaving a trail across her stomach and down to the place between her legs. She smelled like a combination of waterfalls and peaches and tasted like candy. Dro moved his tongue across her clit rapidly, bringing her body to life.

"Sss! Oh, baby! Mm!" she moaned.

He continued the oral pleasure, sucking and licking her pearl tongue like he was trying to get to the center of a Tootsie Pop. When he slipped fingers inside her pussy, she began to shake.

"Oh, God! Oh, my God!" she cried as an orgasm ripped through her.

He moved back up her body, wanting to get in those guts, but she wouldn't let him.

"No. Let me do you. Lay down."

He smiled as he lay back, wanting to watch her suck him off. She began slow, only sucking the head. "Oh, shit, baby," he moaned, letting her know he liked what she was doing.

Forever was encouraged by the sound of his pleasure, and she went down on him some more, sucking him harder. It wasn't the best head he ever got, but it was the best head she ever gave, and that was enough.

A few minutes later he was moaning, on the brink of busting a nut. "I'm about to bust, baby!" he warned.

She stopped sucking and began jacking him off. He erupted a few moments later, coating her hand with his seed.

"That was a lot," Forever smiled proudly, grabbing a t-shirt to wipe her hand off.

"You slayed the dragon, baby. Now climb on top and get you a ride."

She did as he said, impaling herself with his meat. She took her time setting the pace, moving to her own rhythm. Dro moved along beneath her, his hands going back and forth from her breasts, waist, and ass. When she hit her zone, she closed her eyes, digging her nails into the skin of his chest, rocking back and forth.

"Oh, my God! You feel so good, Ruben. I love you so much, baby. Oh, my God!" Forever cried as the orgasm built inside.

"I love you, too, baby. Sss! Oh, shit! Yo' pussy good, baby. Damn," Dro groaned, trying his best to hold back and keep from busting, but her wet pussy was too good. Her moans sounded too good. And her fuck faces looked too good.

He exploded inside her as she came on top of him, wetting his pelvis with her juices. They didn't make a move to separate. She bent down and kissed him, letting their tongues dance. Then she began staring at him.

"What?"

"Is it really over. Are you done?"

"Yeah, babe. It's over. We can leave tomorrow if you want. I wanna be with you and the baby. Let's go."

Forever reached for her phone. "I'm going to order our plane tickets right now."

***

Because of their late night sexcapade, Dro and Forever didn't wake 'til late morning. But as soon as their eyes opened, they finalized their plans to leave as soon as possible. Like, as soon as the next flight left Milwaukee's airport. Dro went home to pack only the necessities and leave everything else to Crush. He called his uncle after leaving Forever's, but didn't get an answer.

After packing a suitcase, he called Shamika.

"Damn, nigga. I was wondering if you was ever gon' get

at a bitch again."

"Hey, I just wanted to call and let you know I'm about to leave town."

She sounded blindsided. "Whoa, baby. Where you going?"

"I told you I was leaving once I finished taking care of everything. I'm done. I'm catching a plane in a couple hours. I didn't want to leave you in the dark."

"Damn, Dro. You really leaving, huh?" she asked sadly.

"Yeah. I'm out. But I just wanted you to know I appreciated everythang you did for me. I fuck with you, for real."

"Damn, baby. I'ma really miss yo' ass. Just know my door always open. I mean that shit. Take care of yourself."

After ending the call with Shamika, he called Crush again. He still didn't get an answer, so he called Candice.

"Hey, Ruben."

"What's going on, Aunty? You seen Uncle Crush?"

"He left early this morning and said he was going by the laundromat. Did you check there?"

"Nah. I tried to call, but I'm headed that way right now. If he calls you, tell him to call me. I'm leaving town in a couple hours, and I need him to look after some things."

"Okay. I'll tell him to call."

Before he could hang up, his other line beeped.

"Hello?"

"Is this Ruben Patrick?"

Dro paused, wondering who the hell was asking for his name. "This is me. Who's calling?"

"This is Detective Hopkins. You own the Pacific View Laundromat, right?"

His heart started beating fast. "Yeah. That's mine. What's going on?"

"There was a shooting on the property. The maintenance

man was gunned down. Can you come to the property so I can ask you some questions?"

To Be Continued...
The Savage Life 3
Coming Soon

Submission Guideline

Submit the first three chapters of your completed manuscript to ldpsubmissions@gmail.com, subject line: Your book's title. The manuscript must be in a .doc file and sent as an attachment. Document should be in Times New Roman, double spaced and in size 12 font. Also, provide your synopsis and full contact information. If sending multiple submissions, they must each be in a separate email.

Have a story but no way to send it electronically? You can still submit to LDP/Ca$h Presents. Send in the first three chapters, written or typed, of your completed manuscript to:

LDP: Submissions Dept
Po Box 870494
Mesquite, Tx 75187

DO NOT send original manuscript. Must be a duplicate.

Provide your synopsis and a cover letter containing your full contact information.

Thanks for considering LDP and Ca$h Presents.

Coming Soon from Lock Down Publications/Ca$h Presents

BOW DOWN TO MY GANGSTA

By **Ca$h**

TORN BETWEEN TWO

By **Coffee**

BLOOD STAINS OF A SHOTTA **III**

By **Jamaica**

STEADY MOBBIN **III**

By **Marcellus Allen**

BLOOD OF A BOSS **VI**

SHADOWS OF THE GAME II

By **Askari**

LOYAL TO THE GAME **IV**

By **T.J. & Jelissa**

A DOPEBOY'S PRAYER **II**

By **Eddie "Wolf" Lee**

IF LOVING YOU IS WRONG… **III**

By **Jelissa**

TRUE SAVAGE **VII**

MIDNIGHT CARTEL

DOPE BOY MAGIC

By **Chris Green**

BLAST FOR ME **III**

DUFFLE BAG CARTEL **IV**

HEARTLESS GOON **III**

A SAVAGE DOPEBOY II

By **Ghost**

A HUSTLER'S DECEIT III

KILL ZONE **II**

BAE BELONGS TO ME III

SOUL OF A MONSTER III

By **Aryanna**

THE COST OF LOYALTY **III**

By **Kweli**

THE SAVAGE LIFE III

By **J-Blunt**

KING OF NEW YORK V

COKE KINGS IV

BORN HEARTLESS III

By **T.J. Edwards**

GORILLAZ IN THE BAY V

De'Kari

THE STREETS ARE CALLING II

Duquie Wilson

KINGPIN KILLAZ IV

STREET KINGS III

PAID IN BLOOD III

CARTEL KILLAZ III

Hood Rich

SINS OF A HUSTLA II

ASAD

TRIGGADALE III

Elijah R. Freeman

KINGZ OF THE GAME V

Playa Ray

SLAUGHTER GANG IV

RUTHLESS HEART II

By Willie Slaughter

THE HEART OF A SAVAGE II

By Jibril Williams

FUK SHYT II

By Blakk Diamond

THE DOPEMAN'S BODYGAURD II

By Tranay Adams

TRAP GOD II

By Troublesome

YAYO II

A SHOOTER'S AMBITION II

By S. Allen

GHOST MOB

Stilloan Robinson

KINGPIN DREAMS

By Paper Boi Rari

CREAM

By Yolanda Moore

SON OF A DOPE FIEND II

By Renta

FOREVER GANGSTA II

By Adrian Dulan

LOYALTY AIN'T PROMISED

By Keith Williams

THE PRICE YOU PAY FOR LOVE

By Destiny Skai

THE LIFE OF A HOOD STAR

By Rashia Wilson

TOE TAGZ II

By Ah'Million

Available Now

RESTRAINING ORDER **I & II**

By **CA$H & Coffee**

LOVE KNOWS NO BOUNDARIES **I II & III**

By **Coffee**

RAISED AS A GOON I, II, III & IV

BRED BY THE SLUMS I, II, III

BLAST FOR ME I & II

ROTTEN TO THE CORE I II III

A BRONX TALE I, II, III

DUFFEL BAG CARTEL I II III

HEARTLESS GOON

A SAVAGE DOPEBOY

HEARTLESS GOON I II

By **Ghost**

LAY IT DOWN **I & II**

LAST OF A DYING BREED

BLOOD STAINS OF A SHOTTA I & II

J-Blunt

By **Bre' Hayes**

BLOOD OF A BOSS **I, II, III, IV, V**

SHADOWS OF THE GAME

By **Askari**

THE STREETS BLEED MURDER **I, II & III**

THE HEART OF A GANGSTA I II& III

By **Jerry Jackson**

CUM FOR ME

CUM FOR ME 2

CUM FOR ME 3

CUM FOR ME 4

CUM FOR ME 5

An **LDP Erotica Collaboration**

BRIDE OF A HUSTLA **I II & II**

THE FETTI GIRLS **I, II& III**

CORRUPTED BY A GANGSTA I, II III, IV

BLINDED BY HIS LOVE

By **Destiny Skai**

WHEN A GOOD GIRL GOES BAD

By **Adrienne**

THE COST OF LOYALTY I II

By Kweli

A GANGSTER'S REVENGE **I II III & IV**

THE BOSS MAN'S DAUGHTERS

THE BOSS MAN'S DAUGHTERS II

THE BOSSMAN'S DAUGHTERS III

THE BOSSMAN'S DAUGHTERS IV

J-Blunt

THE BOSS MAN'S DAUGHTERS **V**

A SAVAGE LOVE **I & II**

BAE BELONGS TO ME I II

A HUSTLER'S DECEIT I, II, III

WHAT BAD BITCHES DO I, II, III

SOUL OF A MONSTER I II

KILL ZONE

By **Aryanna**

A KINGPIN'S AMBITON

A KINGPIN'S AMBITION **II**

I MURDER FOR THE DOUGH

By **Ambitious**

TRUE SAVAGE

TRUE SAVAGE II

TRUE SAVAGE **III**

TRUE SAVAGE **IV**

TRUE SAVAGE **V**

TRUE SAVAGE **VI**

By **Chris Green**

A DOPEBOY'S PRAYER

By **Eddie "Wolf" Lee**

THE KING CARTEL **I, II & III**

By **Frank Gresham**

THESE NIGGAS AIN'T LOYAL **I, II & III**

By **Nikki Tee**

GANGSTA SHYT **I II &III**

By **CATO**

THE ULTIMATE BETRAYAL

By **Phoenix**

BOSS'N UP **I , II & III**

By **Royal Nicole**

I LOVE YOU TO DEATH

By Destiny J

I RIDE FOR MY HITTA

I STILL RIDE FOR MY HITTA

By **Misty Holt**

LOVE & CHASIN' PAPER

By **Qay Crockett**

TO DIE IN VAIN

SINS OF A HUSTLA

By **ASAD**

BROOKLYN HUSTLAZ

By **Boogsy Morina**

BROOKLYN ON LOCK I & II

By **Sonovia**

GANGSTA CITY

By **Teddy Duke**

A DRUG KING AND HIS DIAMOND I & II III

A DOPEMAN'S RICHES

HER MAN, MINE'S TOO I, II

CASH MONEY HO'S

By Nicole Goosby

TRAPHOUSE KING **I II & III**

KINGPIN KILLAZ I II III

STREET KINGS I II

PAID IN BLOOD **I II**

CARTEL KILLAZ I II

By **Hood Rich**

LIPSTICK KILLAH **I, II, III**

CRIME OF PASSION I II & III

By **Mimi**

STEADY MOBBN' **I, II, III**

By **Marcellus Allen**

WHO SHOT YA **I, II, III**

SON OF A DOPE FIEND

Renta

GORILLAZ IN THE BAY **I II III IV**

DE'KARI

TRIGGADALE I II

Elijah R. Freeman

GOD BLESS THE TRAPPERS I, II, III

THESE SCANDALOUS STREETS I, II, III

FEAR MY GANGSTA I, II, III

THESE STREETS DON'T LOVE NOBODY I, II

BURY ME A G I, II, III, IV, V

A GANGSTA'S EMPIRE I, II, III, IV

THE DOPEMAN'S BODYGAURD

Tranay Adams

THE STREETS ARE CALLING

Duquie Wilson

MARRIED TO A BOSS… I II III

By Destiny Skai & Chris Green

KINGZ OF THE GAME I II III IV

Playa Ray

SLAUGHTER GANG I II III

RUTHLESS HEART

By Willie Slaughter

THE HEART OF A SAVAGE

By Jibril Williams

FUK SHYT

By Blakk Diamond

DON'T F#CK WITH MY HEART I II

By Linnea

ADDICTED TO THE DRAMA I II III

By Jamila

YAYO

A SHOOTER'S AMBITION

By S. Allen

TRAP GOD

By Troublesome

FOREVER GANGSTA

By Adrian Dulan

TOE TAGZ

By Ah'Million

<u>BOOKS BY LDP'S CEO, CA$H</u>

<u>TRUST IN NO MAN</u>

<u>TRUST IN NO MAN 2</u>

<u>TRUST IN NO MAN 3</u>

<u>BONDED BY BLOOD</u>

<u>SHORTY GOT A THUG</u>

<u>THUGS CRY</u>

<u>THUGS CRY 2</u>

<u>THUGS CRY 3</u>

<u>TRUST NO BITCH</u>

<u>TRUST NO BITCH 2</u>

<u>TRUST NO BITCH 3</u>

<u>TIL MY CASKET DROPS</u>

<u>RESTRAINING ORDER</u>

<u>RESTRAINING ORDER 2</u>

<u>IN LOVE WITH A CONVICT</u>

<u>Coming Soon</u>

BONDED BY BLOOD 2

BOW DOWN TO MY GANGSTA

The Savage Life 2